ANGEL JUSTICE

by

KEN FARMER

Cover Art by:
Ken Farmer
Adriana Girolami
Cover Model: Stephanie Rhodes

AUTHOR

Ken Farmer didn't write his first full novel until he was sixty-nine years of age. He often wonders what the hell took him so long. At age seventy-eight...he's currently working on novel number thirty-four.

Ken spent thirty years raising cattle and quarter horses in Texas and forty-five years as a professional actor (after a stint in the Marine Corps). Those years gave him a background for storytelling...or as he has been known to say, "I've always been a bit of a bull---t artist, so writing novels kind of came naturally once it occurred to me I could put my stories down on paper."

Ken's writing style has been likened to a combination of Louis L'Amour and Terry C. Johnston with an occasional Hitchcockian twist...now that's a combination.

In addition to his love for writing fiction, he likes to teach acting, voice-over and writing workshops. His favorite expression is: "Just tell the damn story."

Writing has become Ken's second life: he has been a Marine, played collegiate football, been a Texas wildcatter, cattle and horse rancher, professional film and TV actor and director, and now...a novelist. Who knew?

Ken Farmer's dialogue flows like a beautiful western river...it's the gold standard...Carole Beers

ISBN-13: 978-1-7341765-5-1

Timber Creek Press
Imprint of Timber Creek Productions, LLC
312 N. Commerce St.
Gainesville, Texas 76240

Published by: Timber Creek Press
timbercreekpresss@yahoo.com
www.timbercreekpress.net
Twitter: @pagact
Facebook Book Page:
www.facebook.com/TimberCreekPress
Ken's email: pagact@yahoo.com
214-533-4964

DEDICATION

This tome is dedicated to all my wonderful fans throughout the world. Without them, neither I nor any other author would be viable. I hope this fourth novel in the Silke Justice saga meets with your approval.

ACKNOWLEDGMENT

The author gratefully acknowledges Lt. Colonel Clyde DeLoach, USMC (Ret.), Buck Stienke, Terry Heflin - retired English Professor at Tarrant County College, award-winning, best-selling novelist Mary Deal, and Penny (Mom) Tucker for their invaluable help in proofing, beta reading and editing this novel.

This novel is a work of fiction...except the parts that aren't. Names, characters, places, and incidents are either the products of the author's imagination or are used fictitiously. Any resemblance to actual persons, living or dead, business establishments, events, or locales is entirely coincidental, except where they aren't.

TIMBER CREEK PRESS

CHAPTER ONE

SANTA FE COUNTY

A bullet cracked past Silke's ear and buried itself in the bed behind her and Bear Dog with a thud as she drove Luz's buckboard toward town to get supplies. The boom of a long gun sounded a little over a half second later. The black, blue-eyed wolf dog turned and looked where the bullet hit and cocked his head.

Silke was on the right side of the bench seat, Luz sat in the middle, and Haven on the left.

Haven pointed at a ball of white smoke around two hundred yards up the side of the mountain in a copse of piñon pine. "There!"

"Hyaa! Hyaa!"

Silke popped the reins over the rumps of the matched set of sorrel geldings pulling the wagon. Dust boiled up behind them as the two well-trained horses reached their top speed at a full gallop.

Luz levered off three quick shots at the smoke with her '73 Winchester. There was no return fire.

Silke eased back on the ribbons as they rounded a curve and were hidden from the grove of trees where the shot came from.

Silke and Haven Justice were first cousins and virtual look-alikes, including their cerulean blue eyes. The major exception—Silke's long hair was strawberry blonde and Haven's was sable with a few red highlights.

Silke, a female Pinkerton detective, was three years older than the eighteen year old Pinkerton trainee, Haven.

Both had their hair in a single long thick braid. Oddly, Silke's naturally draped over her left shoulder and Haven's, her right.

Silke trotted the pair of geldings into the large downtown Santa Fe Market Square. There were numerous kiosks of local farmers with their produce and Amerindian tribes of Pueblo, Navajo, and Jicarilla Apache selling blankets, pottery, and handmade silver and turquoise jewelry.

Luz McPherson was the sixty year old owner of the horse ranch where the girls were staying, the Bar M. They, along with Bone and Loraine, had brought Luz's orphaned granddaughter, nine year old Elizabeth, out from Texas to her.

A fifth member of the group on the trek out was Reginald Berkley, a mining engineer, who, unbeknownst to either himself or Elizabeth at the time—was actually her biological father.

He had been recently wounded by a neighboring rancher when the rancher's gang attacked Luz's ranch in an effort to run her off because of a gold deposit he had discovered on her property. Berkley was currently recovering back at Luz's ranch.

Luz turned to Silke. "Best we go by Sheriff Russell's office an' report bein' shot at."

"Which way?"

"Turn right up there." She pointed. "His office is only a block that way."

Silke pulled the team to a stop in front of the Sheriff's office, a standard thick-walled adobe building, except the sparse windows were barred with steel rods.

They stepped down, Haven unhooked the lead line from the horse's harness and tied the team to a peeled cedar rail in front of the office. Bear Dog jumped out of the bed to join the ladies as they entered the thick plank door.

The trim gray-haired lawman looked up from the paperwork on his cluttered desk. "Well, what do I owe the pleasure, ladies?" He got to his feet out of respect.

Luz put her hands on her narrow hips. "Somebody took a shot at us 'bout a mile out of town, Case. Around two hundred yards up the side of the mountain from some piñon pines."

"Nobody hit?"

Silke shook her head. "You can come look at the hole in the back of the buckboard. Didn't sound like a .44-40, more like a .45-70."

"Almost have to be for that distance." The sheriff nodded. "I'll go out in a bit an' see as I can find anythin'…know that copse of piñons. Been up there several times gatherin' pine nuts…Probably somebody that knows about that gold deposit on your place…Just need to finish what I'm workin' on."

"Something serious?" asked Haven.

"Could say…Got a rash of teenage Injun girls been disappearin', 'long with two Mestizo an' one white girl…All without a trace."

Silke and Haven exchanged glances.

"Pinkertons were called in to solve a case like this last year up in the Nations," said Silke.

"What was it?"

Silke looked him in the eye, pressed her lips together, then took a breath. "You've heard of the Yellow Slave Trade of course…this was Red Slave Trade."

"So yer talkin' forced prostitution?"

She nodded. "They would be sold to the highest bidder. Each was forced to sign, or make their mark, a document statin' they were to prostitute their bodies for a term...seven years or so, on threat of their families bein' hurt or killed."

Haven brought her hand to her mouth. "My God, how horrid."

Silke looked at her and Luz, then at the sheriff. "Once they became 'sportin' gals' or 'fallen angels' at some bordello or parlor house, they no longer tried to escape..."

Luz interrupted her, "Because they felt sullied...embarrassed to be around anyone 'cause of what they'd been forced to do, 'specially their families."

Silke nodded. "The mortality rate was very high. Most didn't make seven years...died of abuse, disease..." She pursed her lips. "...or took their own lives."

Haven looked at her cousin. "Did ya'll..."

She gave her a wry smile. "My Chickasaw Lighthorse partner, Red Wolf, an' I shut 'em down...uh, permanentlike."

Sheriff Case Russell looked at her. "Do you reckon the Pinkertons can give us a hand? My jurisdiction only covers Santa Fe County in New

Mexico…This ring goes all the way from Arizona territory to Colorado."

"Haven an' I have to go to Denver…she's gettin' sworn in as a Pinkerton. I'll see about gettin' clearance from our regional supervisor, but I would imagine they'll agree."

The sheriff looked at Haven. "Congratulations Miss…Knowin' the Pinks, I'm sure you've earned it."

Silke looked at him. "While we're gone, it would help to list every abduction you're aware of, who, where an' when for us when we get back…Give us a big leg up."

"I can do that…Need to figure out who's takin' pot shots at you, too."

Silke nodded. "Thinkin' whoever it was got a bit antsy."

"How so?"

"If they'd a waited till we got closer, woulda stood a lot better chance of hittin' one of us in that movin' wagon…whoever they were aimin' at." Silke looked at Luz.

"Shot went 'tween you an' me, so could have been either…but I'm bettin' it was me. Everybody what met ya'll is dead now."

Silke nodded. "Point." She glanced at Haven and Luz. "Let's go get those supplies an' need to check on the train schedule to Denver."

An hour after loading their buckboard with the supplies needed at the Bar M, Silke walked out of the Denver and Rio Grande Railroad Depot and stepped back up in the wagon.

"Train leavin' tomorrow at eleven. Two days to Denver. Got an overnight stay in Trinidad where we change trains."

"Beats two weeks or better by horse," commented Luz.

"Uh-huh." Silke unwrapped the reins from the brake lever and popped them over the geldings. "Come up there, boys." She also clucked twice at them.

The horses stepped out smartly from the duckboard walk in front of the adobe building and set off to the south at a smooth amble trot.

"Haven, why don't you take your Winchester, get in the back with Bear Dog an' the supplies... keep your eye peeled on that copse of piñonss up ahead...If they're there again, should see some glint off their rifle when they stick it out to take a shot."

"Good idea, cuz." She crawled over the seat to the back, sat on a stack of hundred pound oat sacks and levered a round in the chamber.

"Bear Dog, jump out an' go ahead of us." She pointed, then looked at Luz and Haven. "He'll know before we do."

The wolf dog did as he was told and loped off in front of the horses down the road. As he came close to the clump of pines the shot came from before, he looked up the side of the hill to his left, stopped on the side of the road and growled—the hair in the middle of his back stood erect.

"Gun!"

Haven brought her rifle to her shoulder and levered off five rapid shots from the '88 Winchester .45-70, before Silke bumped the team up to another gallop.

"Hyaa, hyaa. Let's go, boys." She slapped their rumps three times with the ribbons.

Haven grabbed the back of the seat to keep from falling as the powerful horses lunged forward. She levered off two more shots after she stabilized her balance in the back of the thundering wagon.

Bear Dog darted hard to his left and sprinted up the side of the mountain through the shinnery toward the pines.

Less than a minute later, they could hear screams coming from the grove.

Silke whistled for him after they passed out of range. He quickly caught up with the wagon, loping easily alongside. Silke reined the team to a stop so he could jump back in over the tailgate.

He sat down beside Haven, wagging his tail—his trademark grin showed his long bloodstained teeth.

Luz looked back at him. "He's kinda handy to have around, idn't he?"

Silke smiled. "You wouldn't believe, Luz, think he actually understands what I say to him."

Luz laughed. "Don't think there's much question."

§§§

CHAPTER TWO

BAR M RANCH

"We'll be headin' out tomorrow to catch the train to Denver for Haven's induction…Ya'll takin' out for Gainesville, soon?"

Bone and Loraine exchanged glances as they all sat around the kitchen table nursing cups of coffee.

He looked at Silke. "Well, I said to myself and to my sweet wife...and I knew it was me because I recognized my voice...think we'll stick around. Don't want to leave Luz, Lizbeth, and Reg here at the ranch with just the hired help...What with that shooter around while ya'll are gone. Pretty good at finding snipers...since I was one in the Marine Corps...Plus, would like to help on that slave trade ring when you get back."

Loraine nodded. "Hate slavery of any kind...especially the sex trade kind. It's abominable...Whoever's doing it needs a good killin'."

Bone grinned and put his arm around Loraine's shoulder. "My baby hates any type of abuse, and especially forced sex on children...She's gonna hurt somebody...count on it."

Silke and Haven both grinned, Luz nodded and even Bear Dog woo-wooed and spun around in a circle.

"Be glad to have you. Know what kind of work you do. We'll be gone around a week an' Sheriff Russell said he'd have a complete report ready on every abduction to date by the time we get back."

"Good place to start," said Loraine. "Give a chance to show Haven what detective work is all about…Takes a lotta leg work."

Luz filled Bone's heavy blue earthenware cup with the pot from the stove. "Reg should be up an' around by then…Maybe soon be strong enough to take us out to the ridge an' show us that quartz outcrop."

The 6' 8", 285 pound lawman nodded. "May find there's been some folks up there too…Chances are the shooter and them are the same and are connected in some way with the deceased Ben Wilford, former owner of the Circle W…Berkley said he didn't tell anyone but Wilford what was in the quartz…Just a SWAG, you understand."

Haven looked puzzled. "SWAG?"

His attractive 5'3" Hispanic wife shook her head. "Scientific Wild-Assed Guess…It's a Bone thing."

He shrugged and grinned.

"Oh, just so ya'll know, I'm leavin' Bear Dog with ya'll. He'll be better off here than scarin' people half to death when he grins at them on the train."

The wolf dog pranced on both front paws and woo wooed at Silke again.

DENVER AND RIO GRAND RAILROAD

Bone, Loraine, and Bear Dog stood on the platform and watched the black 4x4x2, coal-fired locomotive as it slowly chugged north out of the depot, puffing clouds of black smoke from her straight stack.

The narrow gauge railroad would pass through the sheer-walled 1,000 foot deep Royal Gorge as it tracked along the Arkansas River between Pueblo and Denver.

Silke and Haven both wore Gored full length wool suits with skirts tight at the waist, and Keystone waist jackets. The skirts fit smoothly over the hips and flared at the bottom in an inverted tulip shaped bell.

Silke's was of a wool blend dark blue tweed while Haven's was similar, but of a forest green with brown. Both were wearing matching small Goorin Brothers hats pinned in a forward-sitting and slightly to the side fashion. Luz had done their long hair in the popular Gibson Girl style. Each also carried a matching wool shawl over their arms for the evening chill.

Their small purses also carried two-shot .41 caliber Remington derringers they had purchased just before leaving Santa Fe.

Their travel carpet bags with their normal armament and trail clothes were stowed in the overhead bins.

What was also unseen, however, were the small Weebly Bulldog 2.5 inch barrel, .44 caliber revolvers each carried in shoulder holsters under their left arms and to the side of their full breasts.

Haven looked out the window at the bucolic but rugged country passing by the train. There were mountains on both sides of the railway and would be most of the way to Denver.

She and Silke sat in the aisle seats directly across from each other on either side of the car in forward facing seats toward the rear.

"Oh, my isn't that somethin'." She pointed at the snowcapped mountains out the window on Silke's side.

The doorway at the back of the car opened and the blue clad conductor wearing a short-billed, flat-topped hat entered. "Listen up, folks. Just a word to the wise for those of you making your first trip north with the Denver an' Rio Grande...Our motto is go through, not around. Be goin' through a number of tunnels an' I'd advise you to keep the windows closed or this car will fill with smoke from the engine...Believe me it's not somethin' you want."

Silke grinned. "Good to know."

The train rocked and click-clacked along the uneven rails as it chugged its way through the southern Rockies. The coal-burner slowed perceptively as it climbed the next mountain with a tunnel near the top.

The car went virtually pitch black as the engine entered the mouth of the near one hundred yard long tunnel carved through the solid rock.

The train exited the north end of the tunnel and as the first passenger car after the express car came into the light, two men with blue paisley bandanas over the bottom of their faces stood at the front door—pistols in their hands.

"Awright folks, you probably figured out this here's a hold up. Now, don't do anythin' stupid an' nobody gits hurt...Jest put yer valuables in these sacks as we pass by," said one of the tobymen as he headed down the aisleway.

The other robber moved down the opposite side with his flour sack. He had two bank bags tied together from the express car slung over his shoulder.

The first man reached Silke and held his bag out.

"Please don't hurt me." She commenced to wail and cry.

"Ain't gonna hurtcha, hussy, jest shet up an' gimme yer purse."

Silke sniffed. "That's all you want?"

The other man had reached Haven and both were watching Silke's antics.

"Said it was. Now fork it over what you got inside."

She dabbed her eyes with her hanky. "Well, if you're sure that's what you want."

Silke unsnapped the closure on her dark blue silk purse and stuck her hand inside. Her eyes flashed quickly at Haven who was doing the same thing. She extended the purse toward the masked man.

Two almost simultaneous loud roars reverberated inside the closed car as noxious white gunsmoke boiled out of the side of both Silke and Haven's purses and filled the confined area.

Women in the car screamed as the two men banged back against each other, then dropped to the floor like sacks of potatoes.

The dark wool vests covering the middle of both men's chests smoldered and burst into flame briefly before the blood pouring from their wounds put out the fire.

Silke slapped out the flames on the side of her purse. "I hate being called a 'hussy'."

Haven placed her purse on the floor and stepped on the edge to crush the fire. "Me too."

The front door opened and the conductor staggered in carrying a short, double-barreled Greener—blood streamed down the side of his head from a gash.

He stopped when he saw the two bodies in the aisle, then he looked up. "'Body hurt?"

Silke got to her feet shaking her head. "Just you." She walked forward, took his shotgun and handed it to a business man in the seat to her right. "Hold this."

He blinked his saucer-sized eyes. "Yessum."

Silke eased the conductor to an open seat and pressed her hanky to the gash to stop the bleeding.

"Ow." He squinted his eyes at the pain. "Need stitches?"

"Most likely."

A man from the middle of the car got to his feet and followed Haven down to the pair. He carried a small black leather bag.

"I'm a doctor, Miss, best let me take a look."

Silke turned to the middle-aged man and nodded. "Be happy to, Doc. Glad you're aboard."

He looked at her cerulean blue eyes, then at the other passengers and finally at Haven. "No, Miss…We're glad you an' your sister were aboard."

"We're actually cousins, but close enough." Haven grinned.

The conductor looked up at Silke. "You an'…your cousin, took those two out?"

"They sure did," replied the doctor. "Cool as cucumbers, the both of them. Had pistols in their purses an' didn't even take them out…Just shot through the side."

"You don't say?"

"I do say, sir, I do say indeed."

The doctor opened his bag and removed a small bottle of carbolic acid and started cleaning the wound on the conductor's head with a gauze pad. He removed a curved suture needle and some black linen thread and handed them to Haven. "Would you mind threading this, Miss? I need to excise some of this torn skin."

She smiled. "Of course not."

He took a straight razor from his bag and shaved the hair away from the wound—then his surgical scissors and snipped some of the skin to clean up the edge of the gash.

Haven handed him the needle and thread when he had the rest of the blood wiped away.

"Thank you, Miss." He looked at the threaded needle. "Just right…This is going to hurt a bit, sir, I'm afraid."

The conductor nodded. "Dang shore beats the alternative, Doc…get to it."

Silke stuck her bloody hanky in the suit pocket of the man she shot and looked back at Haven.

"Ranger Hickman told us before we left Gainesville there were still train robberies goin' on in Texas 'bout every three days an' to be prepared."

She smiled and nodded. "Looks like it's not limited to Texas."

§§§

CHAPTER THREE

BAR M RANCH

"Get all those horses rounded up that belonged to Wilford's gunhands?" Luz looked at the newly promoted fit and trim foreman, Merkins White.

He held his sweat-stained Stetson in both hands in front of his stomach as he stood on the ground in front of the porch of Luz McPherson's large adobe style ranch house. Bear Dog stretched out next to her rocker.

"Yessum…Good thang, too."

Luz cocked her head. "Oh, how so?"

"Some of 'em were gittin' a mite galled from their saddles an' cinches…time we got to 'em." He chuckled. "Acted real tickled to git that tack off, they did…buckin', jumpin' 'round, an' rollin' in the dirt."

"Any of 'em need doctorin'?"

He nodded. "Four…Washed the sores with lye soap an' then coated 'em with wormwood salve. Be fine in a few days…long as nobody rides 'em."

Bone sat next to Luz in a slatback rocker. "Seen anybody around that ridge?"

"No, sir, Mister Bone…"

"Just plain 'Bone', Merkins. Mister was my daddy."

He grinned. "Yessir, mine too…an' nope hadn't noticed nobody. Woulda run 'em off if'n we did."

"Leave them alone if they look like gunhawks and come get me and Loraine."

He turned to her sitting next to him. "Guess we oughta go into town and send Padrino a telegram telling him we're not coming back real soon."

"And about the case we'll be working on with Silke and Haven."

"That too."

"I would suspect he, Faye, and the others would appreciate it…When do you want to go?"

"What time is it?"

"Figured that's what you'd say." She got to her feet.

"Want me to have Shorty tack up Hildebrandt an' Sweet Face?…They're done eatin'."

She smiled at the head wrangler. "That would be nice, Merkins, much obliged…Bone's doing too much fiddlefartin' around to get to it."

"Not fiddlefartin', Babe…Thought it was obvious I was lollygaggin'…There is a difference."

Loraine shook her head and rolled her eyes. "Why me, Lord?"

TRINIDAD, COLORADO

Silke and Haven boarded the train at Trinidad, a standard gauge line that merged with the Gulf and Colorado tracks that ran through Gainesville. The bodies of the two tobymen were off loaded with the local constabulary.

The rest of the trip through Pueblo, Colorado Springs, and then to Denver had the Rocky Mountains on the west side of the tracks and the great plains on the east—a real dichotomy of views.

Silke glanced at Haven as the train continued chugging its way northward after the overnight layover in Trinidad. "Never been this way before, have you, cuz?"

She looked first out the right side, then out the left and shook her head. "Never been out of Cooke County before...This is amazin'. It's like bein' in two different places at the same time...Flat grasslands on one side an' huge snowcapped mountains on the other."

The passengers in the car were a conglomerate of types. There were cattlemen in big hats and rough clothing, drummers in flashy garb, farmers in bib overalls, and ordinary travelers in street clothes. Also included were a couple of soldiers on furlough and two Indians in traditional blankets and feathered uncrimped crown black hats.

The train rumbled and rocked along at thirty miles an hour, its wheels made their normal mesmerizing rhythmic clacking.

Haven nudged Silke. "Look!"

A group of five horsemen topped a nearby hill and rode down to intercept the train. The horsemen galloped up alongside the train, yelling and waving their hats at the engineer and fireman.

The leader of the riders was a large, broad-shouldered man in his late fifties, hair and mustache were salt and pepper gray. Beside him, dressed like a white man, galloped an Indian with cropped hair.

The passengers gathered on the right side of the car to watch the riders through the window as they gained on the train.

An exciting commotion tittered through the car as the people wondered aloud about who the riders were.

A female passenger waved her hanky in front of her face in trepidation. "Who are they? What do they want?"

A male passenger next to her responded, "Don't know, Ma'am, but looks to be 'bout five of 'em...All armed, too."

A large-bellied, well-dressed man shot to his feet. "Good Godamighty! They're probably train robbers...we'll all be killed!"

Silke reached forward to touch the man's arm. "Sir, just simmer down...They aren't train robbers."

He looked at her and wiped the sweat from his somewhat corpulent face. "They aren't train robbers?...What? How do you know, girl?"

Silke smiled. "Because the one leading them, the gray-haired gentleman...is wearing a badge."

His eyes widened. "A badge? Are you sure?"

Suddenly the train lurched as the brakeman hit the brakes, throwing the overweight man back down in his seat.

"'Course I'm sure, Sir, I saw it on his coat...Besides, I know who that is...He's a Deputy US Marshal."

The man's wife patted his shoulder. "See, my dear, no reason to worry."

The train ground to a halt blowing huge clouds of steam from her relief valves.

The marshal and his posse gathered beside the engine, talking to the engineer. A skinny bespectacled conductor stepped down from the front passenger car, walked forward and conferred with the lawman. Then he turned around and reboarded the train.

The passengers remained in a tizzy until the door at the front end of the car opened and the conductor walked in. He held his hands up for silence and the buzz of speculation subsided.

"Folks, I'll have to ask you to bear with us. Those men who just flagged us down are members of a posse after a bunch of outlaws. They're goin' to ride with us a spell so's they can git in front of the gang."

The passengers all reacted with expressions of relief. The conductor held up his hands again.

"We're sorry to inconvenience you, but there will be a brief delay while the possemen load their horses...If anybody's of a mind to get off and stretch their legs, you may do so. We'll depart in thirty minutes.

He walked down the aisle to the next car to give the same message. Many of the passengers got up from their seats and moved toward the exit.

Silke stood up. "Well, shall we? May not have another chance until we get to Pueblo."

Haven nodded. "Sounds good."

She and Haven headed to the back door, and down the four iron steps to the ground.

"Come on, I'll introduce you." Silke took Haven by the arm.

They walked up to the posse as they were busy loading their horses up a cleated ramp of 2x12s that had been thrown up to the door of the livestock car.

The leader had squatted down, packing his pipe as Silke and Haven walked up. He glanced at the two young ladies and rose to his feet as he recognized Silke.

"Well, kiss a fat baby, if it ain't *Kowishto' Ihoo Hommá*. How are you Silke?"

She cocked her head. "How did you know my Chickasaw name?"

The marshal grinned under his big gray full mustache. "*Anompoli Lawa* told me about your initiation into the Chickasaw Hatchet Woman Clan."

Haven poked Silke's arm. "What's a *Kowishto' Ihoo Hommá* an' who's *Anompoli Lawa*...an' who's he?" She pointed at the lawman.

Silke glanced at her cousin. "Oh, goodness where are my manners...Marshal, this is my cousin, Haven Justice…Haven, meet Deputy US Marshal Selden Lindsey…an' *Kowishto' Ihoo Hommá* is my Chickasaw name meaning Red Hair Woman. *Anompoli Lawa* is Doctor Winchester Ashalatubbi, the Chickasaw tribal Shaman…I'm sure you'll eventually be meetin' him, too."

Selden doffed his big black hat. "Miss Haven, it's a pleasure. Silke an' I have worked together several times up in the Nations…along with Marshals Bass Reeves an' Jack McGann."

Haven curtseyed. "My, my, I've heard Silke speak of you, as well as Marshals Reeves and McGann…I'm honored to be in your presence, sir."

He chuckled. "Well, don't know how much of an honor it is…"

"I'm taking Haven to Denver to be inducted into the Pinkertons. She's goin' to be a detective, too."

He grinned broadly. "Congratulations, my dear. If you're anythin' like Silke, you're a reg'lar firebrand." Selden looked at Silke, then back at Haven. "First thought ya'll were sisters."

"So we've been told." Silke nodded. "We have to get back to Santa Fe, Bone an' Loraine are waiting on us…You remember that Red Slavery ring we took down?"

"I do, I do indeed. Vile miscreants…Hung them all, but two, you know."

Silke shook her head. "Which two?"

"Marvin Bubash an' Rudolph Sterling."

"How did those two miss the noose?"

"Friends with pull in the US Senate…Sure miss the good ol' days when Judge Parker was the final word."

Silke nodded. "Bone mentioned a quote once from a writer of western novels in his time, Ken Farmer, who said…'In a nation that becomes too civilized to administer equal and exact justice to evil…barbarians will rule'…So true."

"Yes it is…Now, get this…They escaped from Leavenworth prison three months ago."

Silke and Haven exchanged glances.

§§§

CHAPTER FOUR

SANTA FE, NEW MEXICO TERRITORY

Bone and Loraine trotted their horses into Santa Fe and headed toward the train depot where Luz told them they would find the Western Union Telegraph and Cable office.

They pulled rein in front of the standard adobe style building, dismounted and wrapped their leathers around the cedar railing. There was one other horse also tied up, standing hip-shot and dozing.

Inside, there was a customer leaning over the counter while the operator was recording an incoming message with a stubby #2 yellow pencil. The racket the key was making was similar to listening to hail on a tin roof.

Bone shook his head. "Don't know how in sam hill anybody can listen to that racket and actually get words out of it...I know Morse code, but I can't hear any pattern at all to that."

Loraine grinned. "Think it's called practice, Bone."

The operator stopped just a second after the clicking did, ripped the yellow flimsy from his pad, got to his feet, and turned around. "Here you go, Sheriff...dollar an' a quarter."

The sheriff dug into his vest pocket, fished out some coins and laid them on the counter. "'Preciate it, Percy." He turned on his heel and almost bumped into Bone.

"Hey, Sheriff Russell."

"Deputy Bone!" His gaze cut to Loraine and he snatched his hat from his head. "Deputy Loraine...Fancy meetin' ya'll here."

"Needing to send a telegram back home tellin' everyone we'll be here a while longer. Going to be helping Silke and Haven on a situation."

"Coincidentally..." He held up the yellow onionskin piece of paper. "...that's what this is about. Collecting case facts for them."

"Let me send my message and we'll drop by your office...Uh...Where're you located, by the way?"

"Just a block off Market Square...to the north."

Bone nodded. "Coffee on?"

"Will be."

"See you in a bit."

The sheriff nodded and headed out the door.

Bone turned to the counter, pulled the pad and pencil over to him and wrote out a note to Padrino except he wrote his full name, Jethro Barthelomew Pereira.

Loraine looked around his shoulder. "You know that's going to piss him off, don't you?"

A half-smile creased his face. "Uh-huh…That's the point. He'll think that if I don't rattle his cage that we don't miss him."

Loraine shook her head. "Bone, that makes no sense whatsoever."

"I know…But it is what it is." He slid the paper over to the operator. "Here you go…Percy, is it?"

"Yessir, but how…"

"Heard Sheriff Russell call you that."

"Oh, right." He looked at the missive and wrinkled his brow underneath his green translucent visor. "Sure this is what you want to say?…That you're goin' varmint huntin'?"

Bone grinned. "He'll know."

"Gonna wait fer an answer?"

"Nope…We'll be over at Sheriff Russell's office, if one comes in."

"Be fifty cents."

Bone reached in his possibles bag and pulled out a half-dollar.

"Thank you, sir, get this right out."

"Much obliged."

Bone touched the narrow brim of his dark green John Bull hat. He and Loraine went out the front door, mounted up, and trotted back toward Market Square.

DENVER AND RIO GRAND RAILROAD

Marshal Selden Lindsey sat in the rear facing seat opposite Silke and Haven as the train chugged north toward Apache City where the posse planned to disembark.

"Who are ya'll chasin', you don't mind me askin'?"

"Ever hear of the Bonner-Crossfield gang, Silke?"

"I have...bunch of real curly wolves...Didn't know they ranged this far north."

"Don't normal...Been chasin' 'em most of a month. Thought they could get away from me leavin' the Nations...They were wrong. Got Seminole Lighthorse, Little Elk, trackin' for me."

"Heard he's almost good as Bass Reeves."

"Almost, but you an' I both know ain't nobody that good." Selden chuckled.

"Where do you think they're headed?"

He smiled. "Well, you 'member how Bass always said, don't track 'em...Go where they're be goin' an' meet 'em there."

"Uh-huh."

"They been goin' straight as a arrow since we run 'em out of Guymon in the Strip toward Prairie View...Farmin' an' ranchin' community on the Huerfano River five mile southeast of Apache City...We hear tell their little bank's got a lot of cash."

"They don't know ya'll'er this close to 'em?" asked Haven.

Selden shook his head. "Don't b'lieve so...They hit that little town 'bout six years ago an' got shot up purty good. Think they've got some revenge on their little minds."

"How many are in the gang?" asked Haven.

"Last count...nine."

"Wish we could go with ya'll, but my boss is 'spectin' us in Denver tomorrow."

"Like to have you. Know how you shoot an' I'm bettin' Haven here is 'bout as good. Neither one of you hoorahs much...I miss my guess."

Silke and Haven looked at each other.

"When do you think they'll hit Prairie View?"

Selden looked at Silke and Haven for about a count of five. "This afternoon...closin' time."

Haven nudged Silke. "We could do it an' still make Denver tomorrow."

Silke thought for a moment, then nodded. "Looks like you're a little outnumbered...We would need horses."

"You've got your gear?"

Silke pointed over their heads at the storage bin. "All but our long guns."

"Won't need 'em. This is goin' to be up close an' personal."

Silke grinned. "My kind of chivaree."

"Should be able to rent a couple horses in Apache City."

SANTA FE

Bone and Loraine wrapped their reins around the hitching rail in front the Sheriff's Office and went inside. He hung his hat on one of several wooden pegs on the near wall.

"Coffee's ready. Cups on that shelf above the stove. Most of 'em are clean...I think."

"Wonderful," muttered Loraine.

She grabbed a hand towel from a hook next to the potbellied stove, picked up the coffee pot and filled the cups when Bone set them on the Sheriff's desk.

"Need a refill, Case?"

He shook his head. "Good."

Bone took his cup, blew across the top and had a small sip. He closed one eye and winced. "Huh, like our coffee back home at the police station."

The sheriff grinned. "That good?"

Loraine took a sip of hers. "If you're going to remove rust."

He shrugged his shoulders. "Made it yesterday, should still be fair decent...but then again..."

Bone nodded. "Like my daddy used to say, 'Beggers can't be choosers...Now, give us some background on these Indian girl disappearances, please sir."

Sheriff Russell leaned back in his chair and propped his worn boots on his desk. "Started of a sudden like 'bout two an' a half months ago..."

"What's the latest count?" Loraine leaned forward with her elbows on her knees.

The sheriff dropped his feet to the floor and looked at his notes. "Seventeen Injun, two Mestizo an' one white."

Bone cocked his head. "Any commonalties?"

"Just age...Nothin' over eighteen or under thirteen."

"Where do the most of them disappear?"

"That's the thing, Loraine...Anywhere the girls are alone or in pairs...Been three pairs, so far. They catch the girls fetchin' water, pickin' berries, or piñon nuts, an' such."

Bone studied the top of his cup for a moment and ran his thumb around the edge in thought. "How many tribes we dealing with?"

"Well, there's twenty-three, all told, just in New Mexico...got nineteen Pueblos, that includes the Hopi...Three Apache, the Fort Sill tribe, the Jaccarillas, and the Mescaleros...an' then of course the Navajo Nation...Haven't gotten the information I sent for in Arizona, yet."

Loraine shook her head. "Joy...What tribes haven't been hit?"

"Some of the more remote Pueblos and of course the Mescalero Apaches...They're only 'bout half civilized an' still a mite testy…includes the remnants of Geronimo's band, the Bedonkohe."

Bone nodded. "Of course…They don't want the Mescaleros on their tails."

Loraine pursed her lips. "Only good thing is it's only been going on for a bit over two months."

Bone looked at Loraine, and then at Sheriff Russell. "My third grade math says that comes out to one girl almost every four days."

APACHE CITY

The eight car train slowed to a stop at the small farming town of Apache City, blowing clouds of steam from both sides of her locomotive.

Marshal Lindsey joined Silke and Haven on the platform outside their passenger car. The girls had their bulging carpet bags at their feet.

"You can rent a room at the Colorado Hotel right next door here an' change into your workin' duds, ladies…I'll go down to the livery an' get a couple mounts. Meet you outside the hotel."

45

Silke nodded. "Good idea Marshal. We can leave our traveling dresses in our room while we go take help ya'll take care of business."

Haven smiled. "Lookin' forward to it."

"What I've heard about the Bonner-Crossfield gang isn't fit for genteel ears."

Marshal Lindsey looked at both ladies. "Just so you know…I'm not particularly interested, one way or another, if we take any of 'em alive…Lost count of the depredations they've committed against men, women…an' even children. Plus seems like no jail's ever been able to hold 'em."

Selden set his square jaw, the muscles rippled on the side. "Ain't inclined on takin' 'em back to the Nations."

§§§

CHAPTER FIVE

SANTA FE

Bone folded the yellow sheets torn out of Sheriff Russell's Big Chief tablet and put them in his possibles pouch.

The lanky sheriff got to his feet as Bone and Loraine did. "Have the rest when I get the telegrams from Arizona."

Bone nodded. "We'll stop back by when we drive in to pick up Silke and Haven when they get back from Denver in a couple of days."

"Should have the information in by then. Need to start movin' on this 'fore anymore girls come up missin'."

Loraine looked back at him from the thick plank front door. "Agreed...Have to try and find out where they're shipping them to...and how."

The door burst open before Loraine could grasp the porcelain knob and a man dressed like a rancher strode though. "Sheriff, Sheriff, got a problem. Gotta come quick."

"What is it, Charlie?"

The man glanced at Loraine and Bone, then back to the sheriff.

"It's awright, Charlie, these folks are law officers from Texas, Deputies Bone and Loraine." Russell looked at the Bones. "This is a local rancher, ya'll, Charlie Loftin...Go ahead."

"It's my daughter, Sheriff...she's gone."

"What do you mean, gone?...She run off?"

Charlie jerked his hat from his head, ran his fingers through his dark damp hair. "Uh-uh...No way she'd do that...ain't but fourteen. Went lookin' fer dewberries down to the creek this mornin' 'bout nine for her an' her mama to make a cobbler...Didn't come in fer lunch. I went down there lookin'...found her gallon bucket 'bout half full an' tumped over, but no sign of her."

"Excuse me."

"Yessir, Mister Bone?"

"It's just Bone, Charlie...How far's your place?"

"Less than three mile...Right close to Blanco Creek."

"Can you take my wife an' me out there?"

"Shore." He spun on his heel and headed back out the door.

Bone turned to the sheriff. "Let you know what we find, Case."

"Want me to come?"

"Not necessary. Need you to be collecting as much information as you can for when Silke an' Haven get back...Think we best hit the ground running on this while it's fresh."

He nodded. "Agreed."

Bone made a slight bow to Loraine and swept his hand toward the door as Charlie exited. "Madam, after you."

APACHE CITY

Silke and Haven rode alongside Marshal Lindsey at the head of the other four men, including the Lighthorse, Little Elk, in the posse.

Lindsey motioned to the men behind him to split and go to each side of the town to enter as they approached the outskirts. He, Silke, and Haven spread out as they trotted into Apache City from the northwest.

"Think we beat them here?"

"Let's hope so, Silke...let's hope so. Ya'll tie up on that side of the street, I'll take the opposite. Little Elk an' the others will be in cover somewhere around the bank...We'll walk on down there." He glanced over at Silke's sidearm. "Whoa, girl, you've got one of those hand cannons like Bone's."

She grinned. "Asked him if I could get one an' he sent Padrino for it...When you shoot somebody with it...they stay shot. Doesn't matter much where you hit them with it, either....50 cal, 350 grain bullets."

He nodded. "Dang! Would think not."

They reined over and tied off at the edge of town, easing their cinches off a little before they walked down the boardwalk on both sides of the main street in the direction of the bank in the small town.

The marshal stopped a young lad of thirteen crossing the dirt street. He leaned over to him. "Son, I'm Marshal Lindsey, need you to do somethin' for me."

The teenager in a narrow brim, uncreased low crown felt hat looked up at the 6'3" lawman. "Yessir."

"Now, listen up, think the Bonner-Crossfield gang's goin' to be ridin' into town in a little bit. Need you to quietly go to everbody you see on the street an' tell 'em to git themselves inside somewheres an' stay there…Probably gonna be some shootin'. Understand?"

The young man looked down the street, and then back up at Selden, his eyes were big as saucers. "Yes, Sir!"

"Now scat."

He turned and started running up to everyone on the street—the main street of Apache City was empty in less than two minutes.

Lindsey motioned to Silke and Haven to find some cover.

There was a feed store across the street from the bank. Silke crouched behind the wooden water trough in front while Haven knelt in back of burlap sacks of oats stacked at the edge of the boardwalk.

Selden slipped down the narrow alleyway on the north side of the red brick bank building and stood in the shadows where he could see the south entrance to town.

Thirty minutes later, Lindsey whistled like a morning dove twice to draw everyone's attention. Beside Silke and Haven across the street, there was one posseman on top of the feed store and another on top of the bank. Little Elk was ensconced across the street in the alley next to the feed store.

There were either returned bird calls or waves letting the marshal know they heard.

Nine horsemen trotted into the main street on the south side of town. They rode almost a hundred yards into Apache City before Bull Bonner held up his hand for all to stop.

The thick-necked outlaw turned to his partner, Jermin Crossfield, a hatchet-faced slim man with a slash for a mouth. "Ain't right, Jermin...Ain't right. Looky...nobody on the street."

· Crossfield's black eyes scanned along the building and their tops. "Don't see 'nybody up on the roofs. Mebe jest a quiet day."

Bull turned in his saddle. "Ya'll keep yer eyes peeled...hairs on my neck is standin' up."

"Hell, Bull, you ain't had a haircut in three er four month," said one of the gang members, Chicken Murphy.

He turned to glare at the skinny man. "Watch yer mouth...Ya'll spread out. Jest me, Jermin, an' Red Jack'll go in the bank...Rest of ya'll cover."

The gang walked their horses down the street and stopped in front of the bank.

Bull, Jermin, and Red Jack dismounted, handed their reins to Arizona Jim and Ugly Bob and stepped to the bank door.

Bull looked at the others. "Don't leave nobody alive in there."

The rest turned their horses to face all directions when Bull opened the door.

Selden Lindsey stepped out from the corner with a .45 in each hand. "Far 'nough, Bonner. Federal Marshal…"

Bull turned, drew, and snapped a hurried shot at Lindsey. The bullet ricocheted from the side of the bricks and whined off into the distance.

All parties opened fire at the same time. Guns roared and smoke boiled up in front of the bank.

Marshal Lindsey's shot caught Bonner in the side and twisted him around and to the boardwalk.

The men on horseback spun about looking for targets, firing indiscriminately through store windows.

Silke raised up from behind the water trough and blew Ugly Bob out of his saddle with a slug to the center of his chest. Her .50 caliber's roar was substantially louder than the others.

Haven looked up from the feed sacks and fanned three shots at Chicken Murphy—all three of her .38-40 rounds impacted the skinny man in a line across his chest. Each shot was less than an inch from the previous one.

The outlaw crumpled in the saddle and flipped off the back as his horse panicked and ran off, bucking, down the street.

The half-breed, Maximo Apodaca, wheeled his horse about and spurred the frightened animal toward the alley next to the feed store. As he reached the entrance, Little Elk launched from his hiding place behind a rain barrel, driving his body into the half Apache, taking both of them to the ground as the horse galloped on down the alley and away.

Little Elk came to his feet with his long Green River knife in his hand. Maximo drew his Bowie. The two men circled each other in the alleyway, their knives carried low in a fighting stance.

Red Jack drew a bead on one of the possemen firing down from the roof of the feed store—he fired. The posseman took the slug to the stomach, rolled over the front facade to the canopy covering the boardwalk—he rolled off to the dusty street with a thud, sending up a cloud of dust.

Silke switched her aim to Red Jack and squeezed. The massive .50 caliber bullet hit the outlaw in the head exploding it like dropping an overripe cantaloupe from a three story window and creating a huge red and gray mist where his head had been.

Jermin Crossfield stood next to Red Jack and was covered with a spray of blood, brains, and fragments of skull. He staggered back away from his minion's body as it crumpled like a rag doll to the boardwalk.

"Good Godamighty." He tried to hold up his hands in surrender, but failed to drop his pistol.

Selden placed a round from each pistol in the middle of his chest, not two inches apart—dropping him to the walk like so much wet newspaper.

Bull, only wounded with Lindsey's first shot, raised up, cocked the hammer on his Remington and aimed at the marshal. Just as he pulled the trigger, Haven put a round through his left ear, blowing his brains out the right ear onto the glass bank door following the slug slamming into the wooden door jam.

Bonner's shot caught Marshal Lindsey in the thigh, throwing him to the walkway.

The posseman on top of the bank shot Amos Alvord out of his saddle with his Winchester, knocking him to the street.

Little Elk and Maximo danced around each other, each scoring cuts, before Silke buried her Chickasaw war hawk between the half Apache's shoulder blades as he was preparing to throw his Bowie at Little Elk in a violation of knife fighting protocol. The half breed planted his face in the dirt in front of the Seminole Lighthorse who nodded to Silke, she smiled back.

Little Joe Ascue, fired a wild shot at Silke, hitting the water trough in front of her and covering her with a spray of water, temporarily blinding her. He took another bead—but so did Haven.

Her shot drilled him between the eyes with a solid *twack*, catapulting him from his horse to the dirt.

Arizona Jim tried to turn his panicked animal in the thick, acrid cloud of gunsmoke that filled the street to get a shot at Haven. Selden raised up on his good leg and planted a .45 bullet in the middle of his chest, driving him from the saddle—dead when he hit the ground.

The sudden silence was overwhelming with the thick cloud of noxious gunsmoke hanging like a pall in the street—it was over.

Silke and Haven got to their feet and looked around at the carnage that took less than forty-five seconds. Nine outlaws were dead along with one posseman, plus a wounded Marshal Lindsey.

Wide-eyed faces of the citizens of Apache City began to peek out from cracked open doors. The young lad who had warned the people on the street, stepped out of the millinery shop next to the bank and looked around at the bodies.

"Gol-ol-ee."

§§§

CHAPTER SIX

BLANCO CREEK

Charlie Loftin raised his hand. "That's the creek where she was at down there…Found her bucket thataway 'bout thirty yards." He pointed to the right.

Bone and Loraine dismounted. He ground tied Hildebrandt, his seventeen hand black half-Friesian gelding and she her bright red sorrel Quarterhorse mare, Sweet Face.

Bone turned back to the father. "Stay up here, if you don't mind, Charlie, and let us look for tracks or sign. Don't need anymore down there than necessary...By the way, what's your daughter's name?"

"Sally Ann, it's Sally Ann...She's our youngest."

Bone and Loraine made their way down the embankment through the thickening brush and cottonwoods. He pointed at the ground near the creek.

"There's her tracks where she worked along the bank...Follow them an' I'll go back up the bank a little as we work along the creek...See if I can see where whoever got her came down."

Loraine nodded. "Right...Looks like she's wearing buttonup shoes. Heels are blocky and more narrow than the soles." She pointed. "Must be Charlie's tracks there."

"Bingo!"

Loraine looked up the bank. "Find something?"

Bone squatted down and studied the ground. "Two sets of tracks...Huh? Interesting..."

"What?"

"Moccasins…with full heeled boots or brogans coming behind."

"Indian?" Loraine moved up to his side.

"My guess…" He stood up and looked where the tracks led. "There."

Bone pointed at a large four foot diameter cottonwood around eight feet from the path close to a nice-sized clump of the wild low growing thorny dewberry vines.

Sally Ann's gallon lard bucket that she was using to pick the berries was laying in the trail by the tree. Most of what she had picked were in the dirt in front of the container.

He and Loraine worked their way down to the tree.

"Even I can tell that two men stood behind this tree for a while. The grass and leaves are trampled…four quirley butts ground out. According to Bass, look like Prince Albert…the tobacco is darker than Bull Durham."

"That's a good point, Babe…The Indian stepped out when she stopped at the berry vines…grabbed her from behind. Then the other man joined him...See there." Bone pointed at the scuffle marks.

"Yeah, and I bet one held her with her mouth covered while the other tied her up."

"Pretty safe bet, Babe."

They followed the tracks of the three further along the trail to a spot where they crossed the shallow creek. "Well, let's get our feet wet."

Bone stepped out in the thirty foot wide gurgling creek following some stream-rounded rocks they could step on to keep mostly out of the clear, shallow water.

Loraine followed behind the big man, stepping where he stepped.

He turned and held out his hand when he reached the opposite bank. Loraine jumped the final four feet, grabbed his hand and let him pull her on to the bank without getting her Apache style knee high moccasins very wet.

"Thanks, Love."

They followed the tracks easily up the opposite bank through the woods until they reached the top.

A little further on through the thinning woods, they came to a narrow ranch-style wagon road that curved back to the west toward the mountains, away from the waterway.

Bone squatted down again at the edge of the trail. "Kept three horses here for several hours, judging by the number of apple piles...Put Sally Ann on one and headed off to the west." He looked back at Loraine. "Have to ask Charlie where this leads...Come on, Babe, let's head back...Wait a minute."

"What?"

He took a folded up small paper bag from his possibles pouch, opened it and scrapped a couple of horse apples inside, folded it back up and put it in his pouch.

Loraine nodded. "Good idea. May tell us where the horses have been grazing...Long shot, but a possible."

He grinned. "Good new fashion detective work."

They turned and worked their way back down to the creek, crossed it again, and came out on top near where they had left Loftin.

"What'd ya'll find?"

Bone looked at Loraine then at the distraught father. "Two men grabbed her. Looked like one was Indian, the other white. Took her across the creek to a road…Where's it lead to the west?"

"It's a loggin' road what goes into the Pecos wilderness at the base of Truchas Peak, this side of the Rio Grande…Thick as hair on a dog's back."

Loraine shook her head. "Joy."

APACHE CITY

Marshal Lindsey hobbled out of the doctor's office on a cane the doc had given him. A white bandage showed through the rip in his trouser leg.

Silke held on to his off arm. "Sure you can ride?"

He looked down at her and frowned. "Had a worse place on my lip an' never quit whistlin, girl…'Sides, druther ride Dan. That big stallion's single foot's a lot smoother than that damn wagon we're gonna be usin' to carry Luke's body to the train…"

He looked at some of the town folk still gathering the outlaw's bodies from the street for the undertaker. "Would hurt a lot worse if'n any of those murderin' scum had gotten away."

Haven grinned. "That wasn't goin' to happen."

The broad-shouldered marshal nodded. "Nope...Right proud of you ladies. Gonna send a letter to the Pinkerton home office in Chicago recommendin' a commendation for the both of you...Ya'll saved some lives...'cludin' mine."

Silke brought her hand to her mouth. "Oh, my." She looked at Haven and smiled. "You may be the only detective in the history of the agency to get a commendation before you're actually sworn in, cuz."

Haven blushed and ducked her head. "Not why I did it. The marshal's posse were pretty outnumbered."

Selden chuckled. "Still outnumbered after ya'll joined us...The Bonner-Crossfield gang just didn't have a clue how much trouble they were in...Haw!...Be sendin' ya'll yer share of what bounty there is...once I git it tallied."

Silke smiled. "Not really necessary, Marshal. We..."

"Gonna be well north of fifteen thousand...all told...Purty fair collection of miscreants and ne'er-do-wells. Been after the Bonner-Crossfield gang for a spell...Everbody from banks 'round the

Nations an' Texas, plus the KATY, Gulf an' Colorado, an' the Santa Fe railroads all put money in the pot for 'em…Mind gonna be better'n two thousand fer each posseman."

Silke and Haven glanced at each other.

"One of the perks of workin' for the Pinkertons, Haven." Silke arched her eyebrows.

Haven grinned. "Oh, my."

BAR M RANCH

Foreman Merkins White and Shorty Henry loped their mounts across the big pasture below the ridge that paralleled the road from the north entrance into Luz's section of land.

Shorty's blue roan gelding shied hard to the left almost hitting Merkins' paint when a slug plowed into the dirt just in front of his right hoof. The boom of a rifle sounded almost a second later.

"Sonofa…" Shorty gathered his reins to pull his horse back into control even as he started to crow-hop.

Merkins had less trouble, but his paint panicked also and danced around a moment. "Let's git!"

"Hyaa, come on son."

Shorty bumped the roan's ribs with his spurs and over-and-undered him with his split reins. He and Merkins sprinted their horses to the ridge on the left putting a much greater distance between them and the mountain side on the east—where the shooter was.

They reined up and spun around when they hit the cover of the trees at the base of the quartz ridge.

"Still a little smoke yonder up the mountain side near the saddle." Merkins pointed.

"Reckon it's the same shooter what shot at Miz Luz?"

Merkins looked at Shorty. "Now what do you think?"

"Ain't a real believer in coincidences…kinda like believin' in superstition."

Merkins looked at Shorty. "How so?"

"Bad luck."

Luz stepped out on the porch with her '73 Winchester followed by Martina.

Bear Dog had been lying on the porch but jumped to his feet looking off to the north when he heard the shot.

Nine year old Elizabeth peeked out from around the door.

"Gunshot, Miz Luz?"

"No question 'bout it, Martina. Big bore, too…Like the one what shot at me or Silke the other day…Bet one of yer cinnamon *sopapillas* it's the same person…Somebody's tryin' to pee in our chili."

"I think when *Señor* Bone an' *Señora* Loraine geet back from Santa Fe, they find."

"Let's hope so…'fore somebody gits killed."

They turned as two horsemen thundered at a full hell-bent-for-leather gallop toward the entrance to the hacienda—Merkins White and Shorty Henry.

The two wranglers slid their horses to figure '11' stops in front of the porch, glanced behind them, then dismounted.

They looked again at the mountain to the northeast, loosened their girths so their winded, lathered mounts could get a blow and tied them to a hitch rail in front.

"Ya'll bein' shot at Merkins?"

"Yessum..." He doffed his sweat-stained felt hat as he stepped up on the porch.

Shorty followed quickly behind him.

"...in the big pasture in front of the ridge. Come from the saddle what leads over to the Circle W."

"Who the hell's over there? Thought we kilt all the hands, 'cludin' the owner, Ben Wilford."

Merkins shook his head. "No idea, Ma'am. No idea atall."

Bear Dog woofed, spun around on the porch, woofed again and danced on his front feet as he stared off to the north.

Bone and Loraine loped their horses down the ranch wagon road, through the tall cedar log entry with an iron Bar M hung from the center on chains. They slowed to a trot, then stopped at the hitching rail next to the one with Merkins and Shorty's horses tied to it and dismounted.

Bone looked the horses over and even though their breathing had returned to normal, their necks and shoulders were still sweaty.

He glanced up at the two men on the porch next to Luz and Martina while he and Loraine tied up. "Ya'll been runnin' from bear...or mountain lion?"

Luz set the butt of her Winchester on the porch next to her foot. "Not unless bear an' lion er shootin' a rifle now."

Bone and Loraine exchanged glances. He raised one eyebrow...

§§§

CHAPTER SEVEN

DENVER, COLORADO

The Gulf and Colorado train chugged into the southern outskirts of Denver. It was still several miles to the depot downtown.

A light gray pall of haze layered over the city from all the fireplaces in use. It would disappear in the summer.

Haven stared out the left side of the train. "Holy cow, what a sight. Look cuz...Brick buildings all the way to the mountains over yonder. Never seen the like. Some are five an' six stories...Oh, my goodness, there's one that's..." Haven counted the stories. "Twelve!" She looked at Silke. "Twelve stories tall...How do they get up to the top?"

"They have what are called 'elevators'. Kind of a box or cage people ride in and a motor lifts it to the top with sort of a block an' tackle."

"What if it fell?"

Silke looked askance at her. "Wouldn't be pretty, cousin."

"Think I'd rather climb the stairs."

Silke grinned. "You wouldn't be the only one. The building The Pinkerton Agency has its office in is six stories."

Haven looked at Silke, her eyes got big. "Really?"

"Really."

"Got one of those elevators?"

"Uh-huh."

"You ride in it?"

"Uh-huh."

Haven looked out at the snowcapped mountains on the far side of Denver. "Guess I will too, then…Not that I want to."

Silke laughed. "Denver is over 5,000 feet in altitude…'bout a mile. Used to be named Denver City till they changed it in '81 to just Denver…It's known as the Mile High City. Be a little winded if we climbed the stairs to the top where the office is."

"Why'd they put it at the top?"

Silke shrugged. "Wasn't my call…View, maybe." She pointed at a red brick building a little over a block from the depot. "That's it over there."

The big black locomotive braked to a stop with a mighty hissing and blowing of steam. People immediately began descending the iron steps to the platform.

Silke and Haven, back in their travel dresses, stepped out of the train. Silke looked around and stuck up her hand and waved at a thirtyish man in a dark gray tweet three piece suit—he was not wearing a hat.

He spied the girls and headed their way. "Silke…and I assume this is Haven Justice?" He bowed slightly and held out his hand.

"Cuz, this is Pinkerton's regional manager, Dave Lisk...Dave, Haven Justice."

"How do you do, Miss Justice. Can't tell you how pleased we are to have you on board."

Haven curtseyed slightly and gave Dave a firm grip handshake.

His gray eyes showed appreciation of her handshake. "Have a treat for you both, today."

Silke cocked a shapely eyebrow. "Oh?...Pray tell what are we in store for?"

Dave winked and gave them a wry grin. "You'll see." He reached forward and grabbed their carpetbags and looked at Silke. "Must have brought your sidearms."

She shrugged her shoulders and winked back.

They stepped up into the Phaeton two horse black buggy tied at the curb in front of the depot.

Dave unhooked the lead and fastened it back to the harness of the onside sorrel gelding and got in on the right side.

He flicked the reins over their rumps and clicked his tongue twice. "Come up there, boys."

They stepped out into the red bricked street with a lively two-beat trot and headed the block and a half to the six story building housing the Pinkerton National Detective Agency.

"Whoa, there, boys." He eased back on the reins, laid them across the front partition and stepped down to the sidewalk.

A young man rushed out of the building as they stopped and held the team as Silke and Haven disembarked. "I'll take them, Mister Lisk."

He nodded. "Thank you Tommy."

Dave grabbed their bags again and headed to the front door of the building. Silke opened the right side of the double doors for him and Haven, then she followed.

The elevator door was open with an elderly blue uniformed white-haired gentleman standing inside. "Welcome back, sir."

"Thank you Leighton...Ladies." He nodded to them and they stepped inside first.

Haven appeared a little nervous as Leighton pulled the folding metal screen across the front, latched it and grasped the brass handle on the half-circle plate attached to the front wall beside the door.

"You ladies hold on to those bars on the sides."

Haven didn't have to be told twice as she grabbed the polished brass bar on the backside of the elevator as Leighton turned the plate handle from the bottom all the way to the top.

The elevator jerked twice, eliciting a gasp from Haven and smiles from Silke and Dave as they watched her.

The eight foot square elevator rumbled and shook as the mechanism lifted it up the shaft. They could see the floors and the openings to the different levels through the folding door as they passed.

Haven's eyes showed white all around her clear blue irises when Leighton pulled the handle back down and the elevator jerked hard again. The bottom of the elevator had gone past the sixth floor by some ten inches, he adjusted the handle slightly to bring it back to level.

He pulled the folding door back. "Pinkerton Detective Agency…All out." He looked back at the girls, especially Haven as it was obvious this was her first elevator ride. "Have a nice day."

Silke and Dave stepped out followed by a cautious Haven as she stepped over the threshold, peering through the four inch crack between the floor and the elevator all the way to the ground floor.

"Oh, my." She turned, looked back, and exhaled when she was safely on the sixth level.

Silke grinned. "Have fun, cuz?"

Haven lifted her eyebrows. "Don't ask." She leaned over close to Silke's ear. "Think I peed my bloomers."

Silke giggled.

Dave set the girl's bags next to the secretary's desk. "Just going to leave these here, Mary."

The middle-aged, somewhat dowdy woman with her brown hair up in a bun on top of her head, nodded. "That's fine, Mister Lisk...He's waiting for you."

Silke glanced at Dave as they walked toward the mahogany paneled door with the brass plate on the front.

DAVE LISK
Regional Manager

A trim gray-haired, well-dressed man sitting on the dark brown leather couch reading a Denver newspaper, looked up as they came in the door, folded it, laid it down and got to his feet.

Silke had an almost imperceptible gasp as he stepped toward them.

Dave held out his hand and the two men shook. "Haven, I would have you meet, Robert Pinkerton, Head of the Pinkerton National Detective Agency."

"Oh, my…" She curtseyed, and then reached for his already proffered hand. "It's a pleasure, sir."

"Not at all, my dear." He glanced at Silke, nodded and smiled, then back at Haven, and shook her hand. "It's a pleasure for me. I was just reading of your exploits yesterday down at Apache City regarding the Bonner-Crossfield gang…Well done! Well done, indeed. Makes me proud to include you in the ranks of the Agency." He glanced at Silke again. "And with no less an illuminary than your cousin, Silke Justice…Must run in the family."

His smile spread across his face.

Haven's face turned a bright shade of pink.

"Thank you, sir, that's very kind." She glanced over at Silke. "We were just doin' what had to be done. Marshal Lindsey was an amazing leader."

"Yes, yes, well aware of Deputy US Marshal Selden Lindsey's exploits. You were fortunate to work with a lawman of his stature."

Dave turned to Silke, then to Haven. "Mister Pinkerton made a special trip from Chicago just to meet you and to swear you in to the agency after he read the report of the incident outside of Santa Fe...Silke has met him before."

Haven blushed again. "Oh, my."

Robert looked at Dave. "Well, shall we get to it?"

"Yes, sir. Have all the paperwork prepared, Haven, if you'll step over to my desk...Need you to sign some forms and I'll give you your own copy of our regulations and policies, then Robert will personally administer the oath."

Haven looked over the four page document, picked up the pen from Dave's holder, dipped it in the ink well and signed the bottom of the last page.

Robert glanced at her signature. "Haven Angela Justice...Heavenly Angel...Interesting."

"Silke's middle name is Diane...meaning Heavenly Divine," offered Dave.

Robert smiled. "My goodness." He glanced from Silke to Haven. "Fits...You ladies could pass for twins were it not for the different color hair."

Silke nodded. "So we've been told."

Ten minutes after they had finished the swearing in ceremony and Haven was presented her badge and identification, Mary brought in a tray of coffee, with a bowl of sugar, a pitcher of cream and a small plate of oatmeal raisin cookies.

Everyone sat back in chairs with Robert on the couch where he was when they came in.

Silke set her cup and saucer on a small end table next to her wing-back chair. "I would like to ask a favor, if I might, Mister Pinkerton."

"Of course, Silke, go right ahead."

"There's a situation that has developed in the New Mexico, Arizona, and Colorado area that I think requires our attention." She turned to her immediate boss. "Dave, you recall the Red Slave trade operation, Chickasaw Lighthorse Red Wolf and I shut down last year?"

"Of course, Silke...and I think I know where this is going."

"Oh?"

He looked over at Robert. "We have been aware for about a month of a similar operation that's been going on for the last two and a half months in that area."

Silke nodded. "That's correct, sir…and I'm sure you're aware that the two ringleaders of the Nations affair, Marvin Bubash an' Rudolph Sterling were only sentenced to twenty years at Leavenworth…an' that they've escaped?"

Robert and Dave exchanged glances.

The head of the agency shook his head. "That they escaped, we did not know."

"Marshal Lindsey told me about it yesterday. Too convenient, in my opinion…"

"As in mine, Silke." Dave nodded.

"We would like…"

Robert Pinkerton held up his hand. "Say no more…You and Haven are hereby tasked to take care of this matter before it gets out of hand. The agency has already been contacted by the Department of Indian Affairs, and several sheriff's departments about assistance…Do you need any more help?"

Silke and Haven exchanged looks.

"No, sir, I don't think so. We already have two volunteers in the form of Sheriff Deputy Darrell Bone and his wife, Sheriff Deputy Loraine Bone who came with us from Texas to deliver the young girl and participated in the situation at the Bar M…"

"Yes, yes." Robert glanced to Dave. "We read about them, also…We can't seem to find out much about them until last year. It's like they just appeared out of the blue."

Silke and Haven exchanged quick glances…

§§§

CHAPTER EIGHT

BAR M RANCH

Bone set the paper bag on the small table next to the chairs on the front porch. He turned it over and dumped the horse turds he had picked up near Blanco Creek on the top.

He took out his black Benchmade 154CM lockback knife from the scabbard on his web belt around his buckskin trousers and hit the button on the side. The 3.5 inch razor sharp blade sprung out and locked in place.

Bone held a stick he had whittled flat on one end in his left hand and the knife in his right. He began to spread the round horse scat about on the wood surface and took out his magnifying glass from the crime scene kit he had made.

Loraine leaned over his shoulder. "See anything?"

"Well, yeah, Babe…horse crap."

She Gibbs-slapped the back of his head. "You know what I mean."

"Love gettin' your goat."

"Damn you, Bone, I'm gonna hurt you."

"King's X…I just wish I knew what I was looking at…He pointed at some remains in the fecal matter. "Like this…kinda remind me of witch hazel blooms, and here, some masticated leaves…"

Luz sat in one of the rockers a couple of feet away on the porch nursing a mug of coffee. "Probably Indian Pear…also know as Shadbush or Juneberry."

"What?" Loraine wrinkled her brow.

"It's a low growin' bush found up in the mountains, usually near a seep or spring. Kinda like an apple tree, but lots littler...an' make a small, really sweet blue lookin' berry what resembles a blueberry, but it ain't...Start bearin' in June so it's bloomin' now...Folks like to make jams an' jellies from 'em...The wildlife love it, deer, elk, bear, coon, birds, an' horses...eat the berries when they ripen, the blooms an' leaves...even the bark when it's droughthy."

"Where might a person find it to the west of Santa Fe...say up towards Truchas Peak?" Bone arched his eyebrows.

Luz pursed her lips for a moment. "Most likely close to the dwellin's near the water source."

Loraine cocked her head. "Dwellings?"

"Cliff dwellin's...where the ancients lived...like the *Anasazi*, the prehistoric ancestors of the Pueblo."

Bone glanced at Loraine, then back at Luz. "So there's some up toward Truchas Peak?"

She nodded. "On the other side."

Bone took a breath and blew it out. "Guess we'll take a trundle up there soon as the girls get back...Hate to wait, but Silke'd have a hissy-fit."

A low grumble rolled from Bear Dog's chest as he got to his feet and stared off at a lone rider cantering down the ranch road almost to the hacienda.

Luz followed his gaze. "Do believe that's Nathan Tyree, one of Sheriff Russell's new deputies. Hear tell he just got out of the cavalry."

Bone grinned. "Sits a horse like he's part of him."

The twenty-seven year old sandy-haired, strapping young law officer reined to a stop and touched his hat brim. "Howdo, Miz Luz." He looked at Bone and Loraine and nodded. "Folks...Take it ya'll're Mister an' Miz Bone?...Brought some stuff for you from the Sheriff."

"Git down, Tyree, give that horse a blow. Want some coffee er glass of sweet tea?"

He dismounted and loosened Laddie's cinch. "Mind I take him over to the water trough, Ma'am?"

"Be disappointed in you if'n you didn't...Case shoulda told you how I am 'bout horses...They git took care of first...If you're stayin' fer supper, go ahead an' shuck your tack, turn him in the corral with ours...they's plenty hay."

"Yessum, he schooled me a good deal on that. Said that'd put me on your bad side right quick."

"The man knows me well...Git it done, I'll have your tea when you git back." She got up and went into the house.

He turned and led the well-muscled claybank Morgan gelding over to the trough by the corral, pulled the tack and put him in with the others.

Loraine leaned over close to Bone. "He remind you of anybody?"

Bone grinned and nodded. "Ben Johnson...Even the character name he used in *She Wore a Yellow Ribbon* and in *Rio Grande*...Tyree."

Tyree walked back to the porch where Luz was waiting with a Mason jar of iced tea. He handed Bone a folded sheaf of yellow papers.

"Thank you, Ma'am. Awright I pull me a couple leaves of mint, Miz Luz?" He looked at the flower bed.

"Go right ahead. Like mint in my own tea."

He stepped down, pinched off a couple of leaves and stirred them in the jar with his finger, then took a sip. "Umm, gooood tea, Ma'am."

Tyree glanced over at the small table with the horse droppings Bone had pulled in front of his chair. "Wellsir, don't think I've ever seen that before."

Bone grinned. "You've never looked inside a horse apple, Tyree?"

"Nawsir, not'n my department."

"We're doing a little detective work."

He frowned. "How so?"

"By determining what the horse has been eating, we might be able to figure out where he came from." Bone pointed at the green balls. "These came from a horse belonging to one of the men that abducted the Loftin girl."

Tyree leaned over and looked at the scattered material. "Uh-huh." He pointed. "That's some leaves an' stuff from a Shadbush."

Loraine nodded. "That's what Luz told us. Said it's found up by mountain seeps or springs like near a cliff dwelling."

"Yessum, that's a fact. Seen a lot of it over in Arizona up around some of the dwellin's when I was with the Seventh Cavalry."

"That was Custer's outfit, wasn't it?"

He looked at Bone. "Yessir, still tryin' to live that down. He got 268 good men kilt at the battle of the Greasy Grass what wasn't necessary...Scouts tol' 'im there was over 3,000 warriors massed up."

Loraine grimaced. "It's reported he said there weren't enough Indians in the world could defeat the Seventh Cavalry."

Tyree shook his head. "Huh...right."

"We think the two men that took the girl...one was an Indian...came from where some Shadbush were located...an' we know they headed toward Truchas Peak."

Tyree nodded at Bone. "Where they came from...probably go back there." He took a sip.

"Our thoughts exactly, Deputy Tyree, our thoughts exactly."

"Hunted that area...Seen some cliff ruins."

Bone glanced at Loraine, then back to him. "Looks like you've just volunteered to lead us there with Silke and Haven when they get back."

He grinned. "Yessir...won't be the first time I been volunteered."

COLORADO

Silke looked out the west side window as the train rumbled south toward Trinidad. "Glad Dave or Mister Pinkerton didn't ask what we knew about Bone an' Loraine's background...Sure wouldn't want to tell 'em a fib."

Haven nodded. "That's a jug of cider better left not opened...Still tryin' to process all that stuff they told us 'bout comin' here from the future an' 'bout Lucy bein' from another planet...Sure lookin' forward to meetin' her."

"When we get back...She saved my boyfriend, Ranger Riley Boston's life. Doc Wellman said his skull was cracked an' he was bleedin' inside his head...Lucy stopped it."

"With that layin' on of hands thing like in the Bible?"

Silke nodded. "Wish he was well enough to help us with this slavery ring. You an' me with Bone an' Loraine...Sure wouldn't hurt to have a Texas Ranger on the case."

"I suspect we'll make do."

"Would imagine...Bone and Loraine were police detectives in their time."

"I want one of those crime scene kits like they made you."

"They're handy as handles on a jug."

BAR M RANCH

"Sheriff Russell assigned me to ya'll for whatever you need...He included a note in that packet of paper I brought. I'm to do whatever ya'll say...Oh, there's a telegram in there from Silke Justice. They'll be in on tomorrow's train."

Bone nodded, picked up the packet of yellow sheets from the sheriff's Big Chief tablet and thumbed through the pages. "What was your rank when you mustered out of the cavalry?"

"Sergeant."

"Three striper?"

"Yessir."

"No yes sir. I was a non-com like you but in the Marine Corps...Gunnery Sergeant."

"That's three stripes an' two rockers, ain't it?"

"Is...What was your responsibility?"

"Patrol non-com...eight man."

"Ever serve with a guy named Edgar Rice Burroughs? Think he was in the Seventh, too."

"Sure…Called him Eddie. He was a trooper in my unit. Got discharged in '97…somethin' wrong with his ticker…Know 'im?"

Bone shook his head. "Know of him is all."

Tyree chuckled. "Feller could tell more stories than you could shake a stick at."

Bone and Loraine both grinned.

"Heard…Sheriff tell you about somebody taking pot shots at the ladies when they came into town the other day?"

"Did…He went out to that copse of pinions, found a .45-70 casin' up near the middle."

Luz nodded. "That's what I figured it was…My hired help, Merkins an' Shorty got shot at this mornin'. They figured it was a big bore, too…Come from the east ridge."

"'Nbody hit?"

"Nope, they hauled their butts to the west to some trees to git outta range, then come back to the ranch to tell me…Ain't real sure they're tryin' to hit 'nybody."

Tyree lifted one eyebrow. "How's that?"

"Well, either they cain't shoot worth a tinker's damn…or they ain't tryin' to hit anythin'."

Tyree looked at her long and hard. "Wanna take that chance, Miz Luz?"

§§§

CHAPTER NINE

TRUCHAS PEAK

Ollie Wilkes followed behind *Tai' Múh,* Three Owls, of the *Bedonkohe* band of the *Chiricahua* Apache as he led the way through the fragrant pines, cedar, and open meadows while they descended the west side of the mountain. The dew still clung to the mountain grasses, sparkling like diamonds in the morning sun. There were some vertical light tan sandstone cliffs visible around three miles ahead.

Wilkes led a bay gelding. A fourteen year old towheaded girl, Sally Ann Loftin, her hands tied to the saddlehorn with leather strips, sat in the saddle—her chin on her chest.

Tears streaked the dirt of her frightened face. A filthy rag was tied around her head and over her mouth as a gag.

Three Owls wore traditional Apache warrior dress, a loose white cotton tunic and pants banded at the waist with a gunbelt plus a deerskin breechclout. He had Apache style knee-high, lightly beaded moccasins, laced up the side. A red band of cloth encircled his head over his shoulder length black hair slicked down with bear grease. He carried a worn Army Colt .44-40, stuck in his belt along with a Green River butcher knife and a tomahawk.

Wilkes was dressed in a dark gray three piece sackcloth suit, cavalry style scalloped top boots, and a battered dark green felt campaign hat.

"How much further to that stream, Three Owls? Gittin' thirsty."

"Uhh, *pindah-lickyoee* need be like Apache. Drink water when get camp."

"Damn you, red-hide, tol' you not to call me that *pindah* whatever. Got a name...Ollie Wilkes...use it."

Three Owls spat to the side. "Wilkes no name for man...you better just as *pindah-lickyoee,* white eyes." He laughed, then turned in his saddle and stared at Wilkes with his cold obsidian eyes. "Mebe so *Tai' Múh* kill *pindah-lickyoee* an' take yellow-hair girl for self...by an' by."

"Boss won't take kindly to that. You know he wants to keep her fresh for the buyers."

"Paugh."

BAR M RANCH

Bone, Loraine, and Tyree rose from the kitchen table after their breakfast of thick bacon strips, *huevos rancheros, tortillas,* refried beans with chopped Hatch chilies and several cups of coffee.

Tyree wiped his mouth with his napkin. "Martina, if you weren't already married, might have to be sparkin' you."

Luz's plump Mexican cook giggled and swatted him with a dish towel as she cleared the dishes. "Oh, *Señor* Tyree."

Loraine grinned at them. "Well, shall we go see if we can find any sign where that shooter was that cranked a round at Merkins and Shorty?"

Tyree nodded and smiled. "Been waitin' all mornin' for somebody to suggest that."

Bone looked askance at him. "Noticed that when you were on your second helping of *huevos rancheros*, there, Tyree."

He pushed the curl of hair from his forehead that had dropped down. "Didn't want to have a sinkin' spell, Bone."

Loraine shook her head as they headed out the front door. "Not much of a chance on that...I thought Bone could eat."

Thirty minutes later, they trotted through the main entrance to the hacienda compound and north up the road to the ridge. Bear Dog loped alongside as Shorty led the way.

He held his hand for all to stop and pointed about halfway up the slope to the saddle between the Bar M and the Circle W. "Shot come from there, just to the left of that big live oak yonder."

Bone stepped down from Hildebrandt. "Best we walk up so we don't accidentally disturb any tracks or other sign."

Tyree dismounted from Laddie. "Understand why the sheriff wanted me to spend time with ya'll. Said the both of you were detectives where you came from in Texas."

Loraine handed her reins to Shorty as did Bone and Tyree. "You'll find most detective work involves a lot of shoe leather and an equal amount of common sense."

"Yessum, can see that."

Bone flicked his hand toward the incline. "Go on, Bear Dog...hunt."

Tyree watched him head into the trees, nose to the ground and zigzagging back and forth. "Didn't know better, would think that big feller knew what you were sayin'."

Bone grinned back at the young man. "What makes you think he doesn't?"

"Silke says sometimes he'll do something before she has a chance to tell him...She thinks he knows what she's thinking," added Loraine.

"Can buy that. Kinda like he don't look atchu, he looks through you with them blue eyes...Easy to think it's a person doin' it."

Loraine pushed a limb from a chitalpa tree out of her way. "Maybe he was."

"Come again, Ma'am?" He grabbed the same limb before she let it go.

"Nothing."

Bear Dog stopped under the big live oak, turned around, sat down and woo-wooed back at Bone.

Tyree looked at Loraine. "What's that he's doin'?...Not a bark er a growl."

She grinned. "His way of quietly letting us know he's found something. Sometimes he'll do it if he's fussing at us for something or other but there's a different tone to it."

"You sayin' he's talkin'?"

Bone nodded. "Pretty much. Dang sure know what he means...an' you better listen or he gets pissed off." He knelt down beside the tree and studied the ground. "Well, well."

"Find somethin'?"

He looked up at Tyree, then at Loraine. "Could say...Looks to be that there were two of them. Some small prints and a really big set plus he's wearing moccasins…Feet are bigger than mine an' I wear a size sixteen."

"Was gonna say didn't look like you needed snowshoes."

Loraine giggled. "Ooo, Tyree, that's good."

Bone shook his head. "Ha, ha…Pick on the big guy." He picked up a spent brass from the leaves by sticking his stubby #2 yellow pencil from his pouch inside and held it up.

".45-70."

"Just like the one Sheriff Russell found in those pinions. How come you to pick that up with a pencil?"

"Some more of that detective work, we know how to check the fingerprints of whoever handled it and can match them with a suspected shooter…No two people in the world have the same print…Sometimes the smallest clue or peice of evidence can bring a perp down."

"Perp?"

"Perpetrator, Tyree," said Loriane.

"Huh, be danged…Mind I see that?"

Bone handed the casing to Tyree with the pencil.

He smelled it. "Fresh."

Tyree handed it back to Bone who put it in his possibles pouch.

"Sheriff find two sets of tracks?"

Tyree glanced to Loraine. "Didn't say."

"Small tracks did the shooting." Bone pointed at the ground. "See that extra lip on the heel of that boot, Babe?"

Loraine looked at the track next to the tree. "Oh, right."

Tyree nodded. "The smaller man shootin' that big bore got rocked by the recoil…Big man wouldn't do that."

Bone cocked an eyebrow. "What makes you think it was a man?"

"Ah…Could be a boy…or a woman?"

"Right."

Tyree leaned over and studied the trunk of the oak. "Looky here, bark's bruised where the shooter steadied the barrel against it."

Bone cocked his head. "Good observation, Tyree. Missed that."

A low growl rumbled from Bear Dog as he looked up the incline—the hair on his back rose.

Bone dove to the ground. "Down! Down!"

A slug slapped into the trunk of the tree as Loraine and Tyree joined Bone in kissing the leaf covered forest floor. The boom of the long gun echoed across the valley.

Another bullet slammed into the bole of the live oak lower to the ground before the sound of the first died away.

"Get 'im, Bear Dog," commanded Bone as he looked up trying to see the telltale smoke cloud.

The half-wolf darted through the brush up the hill. He had just disappeared when the sound of two horses galloping off over the saddle came to their ears.

Bone whistled and called out, "Bear Dog."

It was only a short moment before he reappeared from up the slope and came directly to Bone. The big man ruffled his ears. "Good boy." He looked back at Loraine and Tyree. "Don't have time to get the horses for a tail chase...Let's go take a look-see."

"Bet it was the same jackanapes."

"No, bet, Tyree," said Loraine as she followed Bone up the hill.

They worked their way over to the trail that led over the saddle and down to the Circle W, and spread out.

"Got somethin'." Tyree stopped, leaned over and looked under a Douglas Fir and picked up two casings using a twig.

Bone stepped over. "Same?"

"Same caliber anyways."

Bone took them and handed them to Loraine to put in her parfleche so they wouldn't mix them. Then he brushed aside some of the needles to the soft earth.

"Same tracks...Big ones and little ones. Little did the shooting again...Big guy's heavier than me, and I'm 285...judgin' from the depth of the prints."

Tyree nodded. "Figured."

"Whoop, here's somethin'." Tyree looked at the rough bark of the fir. "Tobacco juice...chaw. Guessin' from the big man."

Loraine stuck the tip of her index finger on some of the residual moisture and smelled of it. She turned to Tyree. "You chew?"

He shook his head. "No, Ma'am, don't chaw, don't gamble."

"Bass Reeves could tell what brand of tobacco it was from the smell."

"Huh? That's kinda like findin' a whisper in a whirlwind."

Bone grinned. "Interesting way to put it...Best tracker I ever saw. His old partner, Marshal Jack McGann, used to say Bass could track a fish up a river."

Tyree chuckled and nodded. "Heard tell he's double backboned."

Loraine glanced at Tyree as she followed Bone back down the hill. "Pretty apt description. Bass served over three thousand felony warrants and never had one that he failed to bring in...one way or the other."

"Be nice to meet him one day."

Bone looked over his shoulder. "Could happen...He was my best man at our wedding."

"And Marshal Fiona Miller Flynn was my matron of honor."

Tyree's mouth dropped. "You're not funnin' me, are you, Ma'am?"

Loraine shook her head, her long black tresses tied in a low pony tail swung from side to side. "Not hardly."

They exited the woods back down onto the road where Shorty was waiting with their horses. "'Nbody hit?…Heard the shootin'. Sounded the same as what shot at me an' Merkins."

Bone nodded. "Was….45-70. Two people."

"Two?"

"Big person an' a little one. Little one done the shootin'…both times," added Tyree.

Shorty frowned. "Well, who in the world?"

Loraine pursed her lips. "Need to find who it is."

Tyree shook his head. "Gonna be like putting socks on a rooster."

§§§

CHAPTER TEN

SANTA FE

The Denver and Rio Grande train steamed to a stop at the Santa Fe depot with a hissing and blowing of steam from the relief valves.

White clad porters set extra steps at the platforms for the passenger cars for those disembarking and the new outbound passengers.

Silke and Haven, carrying their carpet bags, stepped down and looked around. Haven spied Bone's dark green John Bull hat sticking above the crowd.

"There." She pointed.

They worked their way through the people to an open area around Bone, Loraine, Tyree, and Bear Dog. It was apparent no one wanted to get too close to the half wolf.

He was first to spy the girls as they approached and began spinning around.

The big animal raised up on his back feet, standing taller than the 5'8" Silke, put his front paws on her shoulders, and began giving her welcome kisses.

The people around moved even further away as they first thought he was attacking her, until she set her bag on the ground and hugged him.

"Yes, yes, I'm glad to see you too, Bear Dog. You're such a baby…Now, get down."

He dropped to all fours and butted her legs with the top of his head, crying in pleasure that his mistress was back.

Loraine hugged each of the girls briefly.

"Silke, Haven, this is Deputy Nathan Tyree. Sheriff Russell has assigned him to us for the slavery case...Tyree, meet Silke and Haven Justice."

He snatched the hat from his head. "Miss Silke, Miss Haven, it's a real pleasure."

"It's just plain Silke..."

"And Haven...Deputy."

He grinned sheepishly. "My friends...an' enemies for that matter, call me Tyree...Ya'll surely do look alike awright."

His light brown eyes held on Haven a little longer than on Silke as they both nodded to him—a look that didn't go unnoticed by Loraine or Silke.

"Wagon's out front. Ya'll follow me." He picked up their bags and led the way to the street in front of the adobe depot.

Tyree helped both Silke and Haven into the bench seat after he put their bags in the bed. He walked around the two sorrel geldings hitched to the buckboard, untied the lead from the hitch rail, hooked it back to their harness, stepped up, and sat down in the driver's side—the right.

Bone and Loraine mounted Hildebrandt and Sweet Face as Tyree clucked to the geldings—they stepped away from the duckboard walkway.

Haven, sitting in the middle, turned to Tyree. "Could we stop at the *mercado?* Like to see if some of the Indian kiosks have somethin'."

"Whatever you wish...Haven."

Tyree didn't notice her studying gaze remaining on him as he directed the team in the direction of the big central market.

He pulled into a wagon yard next to the market square in the center of downtown Santa Fe and halted the team.

A young Mexican boy around fifteen stepped up to Tyree. *"Buenos tardes, señor."*

"Buenos tardes, amigo...Gonna do some shoppin'. Mind waterin' the horses...*regar los caballos?"* He handed the young man a fifty cent piece.

"Si, señor."

Tyree assisted the girls down and nodded to the lad as Bear Dog jumped out of the bed of the wagon.

Silke looked over at Haven. "What are you lookin' for, cuz?"

She smiled and glanced back at Silke. "A war bow."

Tyree raised his eyebrows. "War bow?"

Haven nodded. "Had one back home I got from a Kiowa family that lived nearby. Practiced all the time. Brought in more than one deer an' wild pigs for the smokehouse growin' up."

Silke cocked her head. "Didn't know that."

"Whole lot quieter than a .44-40 Winchester…'course they don't have the range of an English long bow, but they are deadly."

"Fact there," commented Tyree.

They walked along the goods the locals had spread out on blankets and several that had handmade tables.

Haven stopped at one with an elderly Apache sitting cross-legged at the back edge of his capote style wool blanket. His hair was mostly gray and bound by a blue strip of cloth.

Unlike some of his contemporaries who carried generally pottery and turquoise studded silver jewelry, his wares consisted exclusively of Indian weaponry.

He had knives of several types, all with horn or bone handles, steel halberd style tomahawks, along with war bows and arrows, and also lances.

One bow was re-curved similar to an ancient Mongol war bow. Haven picked it up.

She studied the bow and could tell it had been used in battle, not just made for the trade blanket.

The bow was approximately four feet in length. The inside and outside was laminated with long strips of horn from a longhorn steer bonded to the tough, springy, mesquite core with a water repellent glue made from boiling the tripe of an elk, bound with elk sinew, and then sealed again.

Haven placed one end on the ground against the instep of her left foot, pulled the re-curved opposite end down with her left hand and slipped the string, also of elk sinew from the backstrap of the big animal, around the notched end.

The old Apache warrior's dark eyes grew large as he got to his feet. "Uhh, never see woman string that bow before."

She smiled at him. "Had some practice."

Haven held the bow in her left hand, arm extended, and pulled the string back to her cheek, then eased it forward and nodded. She unstrung the weapon, laid it down, and picked up one of the arrows on the blanket and sighted down the length to check that it was true.

Haven looked at the old warrior and pursed her full lips. "Good."

His ebony eyes twinkled. "Had some practice...Me Standing Elk." He glanced down at Bear Dog and nodded. "Spirit wolf."

Bear Dog raised a paw and placed it against Standing Elk's knee.

He looked at Haven, then Silke. "Him know."

The arrows were tipped with steel heads made from whiskey barrel strapping bands, shaped to a point, ground sharp, and bound to the slotted shaft by fine cougar sinew. The fletching was of turkey tail feathers.

Haven held up the bow. "Apache?"

The Indian shook his head. "Take from Cheyenne Dog soldier...in battle. Him no need any longer." His stoic expression never changed but his eyes did.

"How much? Bow, cover, quiver...this many arrows." Haven held up her open hands, fingers spread wide, closed them and opened them again for twenty.

The wily Apache held up both hands, fingers open.

Haven nodded, reached into her purse with the burned bullet hole in the side, took out a gold eagle and placed it in the old warrior's hand.

He looked at the shiny ten dollar gold piece, bit it, and nodded. "Uhh."

Haven smiled and placed her hand on his shoulder. "Thank you, Standing Elk…great warrior."

The Apache nodded, turned and sat back down as the group left.

Tyree walked beside Haven. "Where'd you learn so much about Injuns?"

"Like I said, had a Kiowa family were neighbors back home in Cooke County, Texas. We lived in the Red River valley. Taught me a lot about huntin', trackin'…an' the plains Indian culture."

Loraine nudged Bone, then Tyree. "Look!"

She pointed across the way to the other side of the large market at a huge man in a brown bowler, with long dark hair, walking next to a teenage girl—he towered above the crowd.

Bone started moving in the giant's direction. "Right arm is bandaged." He glanced at the others. "Think it's our shooter?"

Silke looked at Bone. "Do what?"

"Somebody took a shot at Merkins and Shorty yesterday...probably the same who shot at ya'll... Found two sets of tracks along with brass...a small set, who did the shooting, and a giant set of tracks next to them," explained Loraine.

Tyree moved up beside Bone as they hurried across the plaza.

"Could be a coincidence? Think there could be more'n two guys big as ya'll?"

Bone shook his head. "Leroy Jethro Gibbs Rule 39: There is no such thing as a coincidence."

Tyree frowned and glanced over. "Who?"

Bone had his 'I know something you don't know' grin. "Oh, just a...cop guy...uh, back home that makes rules up about things."

The group worked their way through the shoppers and the lookers.

"How many rules does he have?"

Bone shook his head. "Sixty-nine...but nobody knows what they all are."

Tyree arched one eyebrow. "Wanna run that one by the gate again."

"Nobody's ever heard them all, he'll just remind you if you break one."

"Where'd they go?" Loraine scanned the area.

"Don't suppose they saw us an' lit a shuck?" asked Silke.

Bone shrugged. "Rule eight...Never take anything for granted."

Tyree nodded. "Now, that's one I can understand...Best go check in with the sheriff while we're in town."

"Maybe he knows something about that big guy and the young girl," offered Haven.

Tyree opened the door to the sheriff's office and jail and held it for the others.

Sheriff Russell looked up from his paperwork on his desk and removed his wire-rimmed reading glasses. "Thought I'd be seein' ya'll...You a full-fledged Pinkerton Detective now, Haven?"

Her face beamed. "I am. Thank you, sir."

"Mister Robert Pinkerton himself administered the oath and personally gave us the go ahead to work on the slave ring…Anythin' new since the abduction of the Loftin girl?"

He nodded. "Fact is, a Navajo girl came up missin' yesterday."

Bone blew out his breath. "We best get on about it then. Got to find out who's shooting at us at the same time."

The sheriff leaned back in his chair and propped his dirt coated boots on the top of his desk. "More shots?"

"Yeah." Bone glanced at Loraine and Tyree. "Two rounds fired at us yesterday when we were investigating where the shooter was that shot at Merkins and Shorty…and that's what we wanted to ask abut."

He looked up at the big man. "That would be?"

"We determined there were two…and here's the thing. The shooter we think is a teenage girl but there's a guy bigger'n me with her."

The sheriff nodded. "Found two sets, too, in the piñons."

"Seen or heard of anybody fittin' that description in town?…We caught a glimpse of a Indian, probably near seven feet tall with a cornsilk headed girl, maybe fifteen or so, at the market."

Russell whistled. "Seven feet...sounds like an Osage, Bone."

Bone looked at Loraine. "Heard they can be like ghosts."

Tyree shook his head. "Doesn't matter if'n he's a hippopotamus, one of them go-rillas, or a haint...need to get on about it an'find 'em 'fore they're successful an' hit Miz Luz, so's we can git after them girls."

Haven glanced at Silke. "Looks like we're fightin' the clock on both, cuz."

§§§

CHAPTER ELEVEN

SANTA FE

Tyree popped the reins over the team. "Come up there, boys." He directed them out the south road toward the Bar M ranch.

Silke and Haven sat beside him on the bench, Haven in the middle. Bone and Loraine trotted along behind with Bear Dog riding in the back of the buckboard sitting on bags of horse oats they had picked up at the feed store.

They rounded the first curve out of town when Silke was the first to notice the two riders ahead. "Bone!"

He glanced up along with Loraine to see the giant and the young girl trotting their horses south less than fifty yards ahead of them.

Bone clicked twice at Hildebrandt and bumped his ribs with the heels of his moccasin-clad feet. "Come on, son."

The seventeen hand gelding responded with a lunge to a full gallop in a couple of strides with Loraine right on his heels with her mare, Sweet Face.

The girl turned in her saddle at the sound of the pounding hooves—she and the giant Indian spurred their own mounts into a gallop.

Loraine's smaller and lighter mare quickly caught and passed Bone's larger horse. She rapidly gained on the girl and her companion.

The four horses raced down the rutted dirt road leading south from Santa Fe with Tyree encouraging his team to stay with them.

The girl's long cornsilk hair streamed in the breeze behind her. The giant Indian's grula horse couldn't match the speed of the teen or Loraine's mare as she quickly passed him and closed on the girl's red and white paint gelding.

Loraine leaned over like a rodeo pickup rider, snatched the reins from the girl's hands, rotated her hips, and pulled Sweet Face to a sliding stop, effectively halting the paint, too.

"Let go! Turn loose of my horse!" The girl struck at Loraine but couldn't reach her.

Bone and the teen's companion arrived at the same time.

The giant Indian dove from his horse at Bone, taking him from his saddle to the ground before their mounts had completely stopped.

The two behemoths rolled over several times before they came to a complete stop as the dust from the road boiled up around them. They quickly untangled from each other and jumped to their feet.

The seven foot Osage shoved Bone backward forcefully. "White man stay away from her."

Bone held up his hands. "Hey, hey, just want to…"

The Indian didn't wait for Bone to finish before he leg swept him to the ground and jumped on top of him.

Bone twisted around, managed to throw the bigger man off and get to his feet. "Guess this is the way it's going to be." He drove a hard left jab at the Indian's face.

The man lowered his head so Bone's fist hit him in the forehead and bounced off.

"Ow!" Bone shook his hand from the pain.

The Indian looked unfazed and swung a huge right at Bone, catching him alongside his head causing him to see stars.

Bone backed away, blinking his eyes and trying to get his wits back.

The Indian charged and grappled him around his waist, pinning both arms to his sides—he lifted and squeezed Bone in a massive bear hug.

Bone threw his head back and cried out, as his breath was forced from him. "Ahhhh!"

The Osage had Bone's 285 pounds completely off the ground and was literally crushing the life from him.

Bone saw stars again and his vision began to go black from lack of oxygen before he drove his head forward with all his remaining strength, smashing the Indian in the face.

Blood spattered from the Osage's nose as the cartilage broke and more blood squirted down onto Bone.

He loosened his grip when Bone drove his forehead forward once more slamming into his nose.

The giant released Bone, staggered back and shook his head. His ebony eyes glared as he swung another ham-like fist at Bone, again impacting the side of his head.

Bone spun around like a top, but drove his left into the Osage's solar plexus as he came back.

Air whooshed from the Indian's mouth. "Ahhh." He leaned over.

Bone threw a tremendous uppercut to his jaw rocking him back—but he somehow stayed on his feet to swing a mighty kick to Bone's ribs.

Both men went to their knees, facing one another. They traded blows, tit for tat, slower and slower, until neither could raise his hands any longer.

The two men fell forward, collapsing in the dirt almost on top of one another—there was no further movement.

"Bone!" Loraine jumped from Sweet Face and ran to his side.

The young girl did the same from her paint. "*Enah Mahah*!" She knelt beside the groggy Osage.

Bone raised his head and looked at the Indian through swollen eyes. "Had enough?"

The giant nodded and wheezed. "*Enah Mahah* have enough."

Loraine looked over at the teen. "What does *Enah Mahah* mean?"

Tears rolled down her cheek as she cradled his head in her lap. "It's his name. In English it means, Gentle Sky."

Bone tried to shake his head and winced at the pain. "Gentle Sky? That's an enigma inside a paradox wrapped in a contradiction if I ever heard one."

Loraine fetched her canteen from her saddle and held it to Bone's lips. He took several long drafts, then nodded to Gentle Sky.

She handed the canteen to the girl who gave some of the water to her companion. He also took a couple of long swallows and looked at Loraine with gratitude.

"White man hit hard."

Bone grinned through puffy lips. "You don't do too bad yourself...Gentle Sky, my foot."

Loraine looked at the girl. "Who are you?"

"My name is Sarah Wilford...Ben Wilford was my father. Ya'll killed him...I was off at boarding school when the undertaker sent me a telegram."

Loraine raised an eyebrow. "Is that why you've been shooting at us?"

Sarah pinched her lips together and nodded. "Not a very good shot."

Bone sat up with a groan. "You think?"

"An' I wouldn't let Gentle Sky do it."

"He your body guard or something?"

She nodded again. "Father wouldn't let me go off to school without him to watch over me."

"He danged sure makes a good protector, I'll say that."

Loraine put her hand on Sarah's shoulder. "Think you need to hear the full story." She looked at Bone, then at Gentle Sky. "They don't need to be riding their horses, we'll put them in the back of the wagon and go to the Bar M…Believe Luz can fill in some of the holes."

Tyree got down and helped Bone, then Gentle Sky into the back of the wagon on top of the oat sacks.

Loraine tied their horses to the iron rings on the tailgate and remounted her mare.

"Want to leave that canteen with us, Babe? Think me an' my buddy, Gentle Sky here, could use some more." He looked at the Osage.

He nodded. "Uhh."

BAR M RANCH

Two hours later, the wagon pulled into the Bar M. Tyree drew rein in front of the hacienda as Shorty came down from the porch.

"Want me to take 'em, Tyree?"

"Yeah, Shorty, gotta unload the supplies an' horse feed…not countin' the near seven hundered pounds of meat."

"Meat?…Oh, I git it. Bone an' that big feller with him…Huh. Never thought I'd be sayin' that." He laughed.

Everyone got down as Luz came out the front door. "Well, who do we have here?"

Silke and Haven pulled their bags from the back.

"Got our shooter, Luz."

"Do what?" She looked at the girl and the giant Indian.

Silke grinned. "Tell you in a few minutes…Gonna scream if I don't get out of this dress an' in my buckskins."

"Me too," added Haven.

Merkins joined Shorty, took the horses over to the corral to strip their tack, give them a rubdown and turn them in with some hay.

The girls had changed clothes and everyone was on the porch with an ice tea. Loraine and Sarah were tending to Bone and Gentle Sky's bruises, scrapes, and facial cuts.

Luz shook her head. "Never in my life seen two men beat up worse than ya'll."

"Ought to look at us from our side…Feels like it looks, too," said Bone.

"An' man mountain there's name is for sure an' be damned, Gentle Sky?"

Sarah shrugged and nodded. "Yessum, Miz Luz…He really is gentle…unless he's protecting me…He's been with me all my life."

Tyree shook his head. "Hate to be the young lad that tries sparkin' you."

She smiled. "He knows when it's all right with me or not." Sarah looked at Bone and Loraine. "He thought ya'll meant me harm."

Luz took a sip of her tea. "Well, like I told you while the girls were changin', your papa got the gold fever 'bout that deposit on my place an' tried to run me off with a bunch of gunhawks when I refused to sell…We had to defend ourselves, simple as that."

Sarah nodded. "I can understand. Daddy was a hard man, sometimes a bit of a bully, and always wanted things his way. I had no desire to go off to boarding school, but he insisted." She looked off at the distant mountains. "Maybe if I'd been here I could have…"

Luz shook her head. "Not likely, honey. Once the fever hits a man, there's no controllin' it."

"I can vouch for that."

They looked around to the doorway at Reginald Berkley standing there with nine year old Elizabeth holding his hand…

§§§

CHAPTER TWELVE

VALLES CALDERA

Coon Creede and the Comanche half-breed, Shadow Welch, rode into the box canyon on the west side of the giant ancient caldera. The near fourteen mile wide depression in the Jemez Mountains was created when an active volcano collapsed into its magma chamber some 1.2 million years earlier during the Pleistocene Epoch.

Numerous hot springs, pools, streams, fumaroles, gas seeps, grass valleys, and small volcanic domes proliferated the rugged caldera floor. Scattered lava flows and obsidian outcrops abounded.

The northeast facing wall included the ruins of a thousand year old cliff dwelling thirty feet up from the floor of the canyon. The guard at the entrance had waved them through the narrow brush-choked opening.

The two members of the gang were leading another horse with a thirteen year old Navajo girl tied to the saddle. Her face exhibited several bruises but her dark brown eyes showed no capitulation and stared stoically straight ahead— her head up.

There were a number of other men gathered around a campfire several yards away from the cliff face, drinking coffee and smoking, including Ollie Wilkes, Three Owls, Tater Adams, Jess Shepherd, and Hardy Redding. The other remaining two members, Grover Red Hammer and Moose Welch were not back with their assigned target.

"'Bout time ya'll showed up," said Marvin Bubash as he walked over from a large off-white military style four man tent with a table and two chairs out front.

He was dressed in jodhpur khaki pants and a short khaki jacket over a white boiled cotton shirt and a dark red kerchief around his neck. Bubash also wore a brown wide-brim fedora.

Coon Creede glanced at his half-breed partner. "Sorry, boss, she weren't too anxious 'bout leavin' her baby brother." He chuckled. "Till we chunked his little brown ass in the creek an' chased her down when she come back to save him."

"No one saw you?"

"Nope…Nice thing 'bout these Injun gals, they don't scream bloody-murder when they's bein' took like them white split-tails."

"She get the kid out of the creek?"

Creede looked at Shadow again. "Sonofagun, breed, knew we fergot somethin'…Haw."

"Get her up with the others."

Shadow Welch dismounted, ground-tied his bay gelding, grabbed the long cedar pole ladder lying at the base of the cliff and propped it against the wall at the bottom of a doorway in the adobe thirty feet up.

Coon untied the girl's hands from the saddlehorn, pulled her from the horse and led her to the ladder. "Up girlie…Climb."

She jerked her arm from his grasp, gave him the stink-eye, and ascended the ancient style device.

Coon removed the ladder when the maiden stepped inside the opening and laid it back down at the base of the cliff.

Rudolph Sterling, the other organizer, dressed similarly to Bubash except for wearing a dark green tweed jacket, belted in the back, dismounted from the Tennessee sorrel he had ridden into the hideout.

Marvin looked at the older man. "Well?"

"The buyers will meet us at the usual place at San Antonio Mountain in six days for the auction."

BAR M RANCH

"How are you feeling, Reg?" Luz got to her feet and pulled the last empty rocker over for him to sit in.

He smiled. "Lot better than I was…I've had a good nurse." Reg hugged Elizabeth, his new found daughter, to him.

The little blonde-headed girl put both hands on her hips, then raised her right and wagged her index finger at him. "An' you don't mind very well…Papa." She grinned.

"Like some tea?"

He nodded. "That would be nice, Luz."

Bone glanced at Sarah. "This is Reg Berkley, he's a mining engineer your dad hired to come in and verify that the samples his men had collected from Luz's ridge over yonder fact, contained gold…"

"Which he did…" interrupted Silke. "…before he found out he knew Luz back in New York an' that her granddaughter was actually his own daughter that he knew nothing about."

Luz nodded. "Your daddy shot him in the back when he tried to leave his group and go to help me."

"I'm so sorry." Sarah reached over and laid her hand on Reg's arm.

Bone groaned and put his hand on his ribs. "That's when all hell…pardon the expression…broke loose, and when the smoke cleared, your father and all ten of his gunhawks lay on the ground…"

Loraine picked up the story, "We took Mister Berkley inside and treated his wound." She looked at him. "This is the first day he's been out of bed."

"I'm so glad you're feeling better, Mister Berkley and again, I must apologize for my father."

He nodded. "Out of your control, Miss. He was what he was…The good thing that came out of all this was that I got to meet a daughter I had no idea existed." Reg reached over and squeezed Elizabeth's hand. "What are your plans now?"

Sarah took a breath. "My father did work hard to build his ranch and I suppose it's up to me, now, to run it." She looked at the giant Osage. "With Gentle Sky's help…We have already hired one wrangler and need some more." Sarah pursed her lips. "I'm afraid I don't know too much about raising horses."

Luz smiled at the teen. "Truth be known, your father didn't know much about breedin' good bloodlines anyway…I'll be glad to help you there. I'll send one of my hands, Pablo, over till you find some more hands."

"All help will be appreciated, Miz Luz."

"What neighbors are for."

"Yes, Ma'am." Sarah glanced to the Osage. "Do you feel up to riding back to the ranch, Gentle Sky?"

"Uhh, *Enah Mahah*, can ride." He rose painfully to his feet.

She watched him. "Sure?"

"Uhh. Me feel better."

Sarah arched her eyebrows at him as she also got up. "You say so."

Martina brought a small basket out of the house and handed it to Sarah. "Miz Luz asked I fix this for you...Tortillas, beans with meat an' salsa."

"Why, thank you, Martina. I'm sure we'll enjoy it for supper."

Merkins and Shorty brought their horses over to the porch, having saddled them after they'd eaten.

The foreman assisted bruised Gentle Sky a little to mount his horse.

Sarah repositioned the saddle on her paint to the right after sitting down. "Again, I want to thank you for the hospitality and clearing up the story for me...I'm so happy that I'm such a terrible shot. It would have been a terrible, terrible mistake to have hit anyone."

Luz grinned. "Wouldn't have cared too much for it ourselves...I'll send Pablo over soon as he gets in from checkin' the pastures."

Sarah smiled, nodded, turned her gelding about and waved good bye as she and Gentle Sky trotted out the gate.

VALLES CALDERA

Sally Ann Loftin looked around the dim confines of the ancient cliff dwelling 15 x 15 foot room. The only light came from the opening by which they had entered.

She could count nine other girls in the shadows scattered around what could have once been a sleeping room from where she sat, arms around her knees, in a corner.

The latest arrival sat down next to her. "Me Yellow Bird...Navajo."

"Sally Ann."

"How long you here?"

"Two days, but seems longer."

"They do anythin'?"

Sally shook her head. "They seem to want us untouched for some men that want to bid on us like cattle or slaves."

Yellow Bird shook her head. "No *like* slaves...are slaves. Kiowa once did same to my people, but make women part of tribe when stolen."

Sally Ann's voice got soft, "Don't think that's what they have in mind for us."

Yellow Bird glanced at the opening. "Any way get out?"

Sally shook her head. "Too far to the ground an' there's always someone watchin'. Their campfire is always bright enough to light the wall of this cliff."

The Navajo looked at Sally Ann. "Meby best kill ourselves."

Sally frowned. "How?"

BAR M RANCH

Gentle Sky led the way up the mountain to the dip between two hogbacks—their horses climbed at a walk. Sarah could occasionally hear the big man grunt with the movement of the horse.

"Do you want to stop an' rest, Sky?"

He turned in his saddle to look at her—the torquing of his body obviously painful to his cracked ribs. "Only if Sarah need stop."

She shook her head. "No, I'm fine." *I know he'd never be able to get back up in the saddle.*

They followed the trail slowly as it zigzagged through the pines and shaky aspen down the east face of the saddle in the ridge between the Circle W and the Bar M.

The two riders exited the trees into the lush wide grass meadow coulee at the bottom. A number of the Circle W mares grazed contentedly in the belly high mountain grasses.

Abruptly the stallion of the herd snapped his head up and snorted loudly as he stared off to the north.

Gentle Sky eased his Yellow Boy from the scabbard on the side of his saddle as he reined his big grula to a stop. "Sarah go back in trees."

He scanned the meadow to the north, then looked at the tree line as two riders bolted from their cover less than twenty yards away. Both had their Colts palmed.

"Hold it up right there, Injun...Ease that shooter back in the boot, you don't want that little girl to git hurt."

Gentle Sky didn't move his hands from his Winchester. "What white men want?"

"Funny you should ask, Injun. Was jest gonna tell you." He looked at his companion who had spread off to the side another ten feet. "Think we oughta tell 'im, Moose?"

"Nah, Red, think he kin figger it out."

"Yeah, probably right...Got to a count of three, Redhide, to turnaloose that shooter...One..."

Gentle Sky jerked the rifle up, levering a round in the chamber as he did.

Grover Red Hammer and Moose Welch each squeezed off two rapid shots from their .44-40s. All four impacted Gentle Sky's massive chest with audible thumps just as he brought the rifle to a firing position and pulled the trigger.

The five thunderclaps echoed up and down the valley as Sarah screamed...

§§§

CHAPTER THIRTEEN

BAR M RANCH

Luz sat at the head of the table as everyone finished the supper of pork *pozole* and beef enchiladas, all expertly prepared by her long time cook, Martina Gonzales.

Berkley wiped his mouth with his white linen napkin. "I must say, Martina, this supper was exceptional, not to say anything about getting to eat at the table instead of my bed."

"Gracias, *Señor*." She blushed under her dark Mexican skin as she cleared the dishes.

Luz got to her feet, fetched the coffee pot and went around the table, filling everyone's cups except Elizabeth, who had buttermilk.

She glanced at Bone as she topped his off. "How are you feelin' now, Bone?"

He smiled. "Hurt all over more than anywhere else but it's a whole lot better than it was when we rode up…Never had a beating quite like that…and dang sure don't want any more of 'em."

"Looked like you gave as good as you got." She set the pot back on the hot pad.

Loraine patted his shoulder.

"Ow, Babe."

She grinned. "Think ya'll can call it a draw, dear."

"I would laugh but it hurts too much…That's the thing about havin' banged up ribs. Don't laugh, don't cough an' for God's sake…don't sneeze."

Martina came back into the dining room with a white ceramic mug, similar to the one he was drinking coffee from. "*Señor* Bone, you drink thees. Will help."

He looked at the steam rising from the liquid. "What is it, Martina?"

"White willow bark tea. Will help pain."

"Oh, heard about that before…I'll take a gallon." Bone picked it up and took a long sip. "Well, a little bitter but otherwise not too bad."

Silke looked at him from across the table. "Think you'll be able to ride tomorrow?…Need to get on the trail of those girls."

"I would think. Found out when I played football that workin' out or exercising the next day was the best medicine."

Berkley set his cup down. "Is that American football or rugby football like in Great Britain?"

"American…not quite as rough as rugby. Got more pads but still tough."

"American football is big in the east…like at Rutgers, Princeton, Harvard, Dartmouth, the military academies, Army and Navy. Where did you play?"

"Uh…"

"Come queeck! Come queeck!" Pablo rushed into the dining room from the front door.

"What is it, Pablo?" Luz got back to her feet.

"Beeg Indian...outside. I bring. Come queeck!"

Everyone got to their feet and rushed to the front porch.

Gentle Sky was slumped over in his saddle, blood stained both sides of his grula.

"Pablo find horse with big man in saddle coming down trail over mountain to Circle W...I bring."

Tyree rushed up to the horse. "He's unconscious but alive. How in sam hill did he stay in the saddle?...Been shot...a bunch...blood everwhere."

He grabbed Gentle Sky's arm and eased him to the side. Bone, Pablo, Loraine, and Shorty helped pull him from the saddle. Everyone grabbed a limb, Loraine held his head as they carried the blood drenched Osage up the steps.

Luz led the way. "Bring him this way. Damn good thing got plenty of bedrooms...May have to open a hospital."

Loraine, still cradled his head. "Oh, my goodness, I can count four holes in his chest...How's he still alive?"

Bone glanced back at his wife. "I can tell you that, Babe...Because he's Gentle Sky...an' one tough son of a bitch."

"Pablo, did you see the young girl?"

"No, *Señor* Bone, no sign."

Bone and Loraine exchanged glances.

"Uh-oh," muttered Silke.

Luz looked at her hired hand. "Pablo, when we get him on a bed, need you to saddle up a fresh horse an' ride to town for the doc...Matter of fact, take two an' you can swap out without killin' 'em."

He nodded. "*Si, Señora.*"

They laid his seven foot frame on a bed in another of Luz's guest rooms. His feet hung off the foot. She pulled a cedar chest over to the bottom where Bone picked his feet up and placed them on top of the chest.

"I'll go get my kit." Bone left the room.

Haven looked over at the big Indian. "Is he still breathin'?"

Loraine held her fingertips under his nose. "Barely." She checked his pulse from his carotid artery. "Low and slow...and erratic.'

Loraine and Silke immediately began cutting his completely saturated shirt and pants from his body with the scissors furnished by Luz before she left the room to get towels.

She yelled down the hallway, "Martina! Boil water…lots of it."

Luz grabbed a stack of towels from the linen closet in the hall and hurried back to the room entering just behind Bone.

Silke and Haven quickly grabbed a towel each and cleaned the excess blood from the giant man's chest.

"My God, Loraine, you were right…four holes. Look like .45 or close to it."

"Any pass through, Silke?"

"Gonna need some help to turn him over a bit to see."

Tyree and Bone rolled him slightly to his left shoulder.

"Three through and throughs," said Silke.

"See any bubbles?" asked Loraine.

Bone leaned over to study the exit wounds on his back. "Don't think so, Babe…but he's lost a lot of blood."

Bone and Tyree eased him back down after Haven had sprinkled some of Bone's alum powder from his kit in the wounds to stop the bleeding and placing pads made from a torn up towel on each one.

Luz headed back out the door. "I'll go get some honey and tequila."

Loraine shook her head. "Seems we did this not too long ago." She glanced over at Berkley who was standing just inside the door with Elizabeth.

He smiled. "And a good job you did, too."

"Oh, God! He's stopped breathin'." Loraine felt for a pulse and looked at Bone. "Nothing."

VALLES CALDERA

"Damn redhide bounced a ball off'n my ribs. Hurts like hell." Grover Red Hammer held his kerchief over the spreading red area on his side.

Moose Welch, led Sarah's paint. Her hands were tied to her saddlehorn.

"You'll git over it...Beats the alternative anyhoo, don't it?"

"Cain't believe the big bastard didn't fall outta the saddle."

"You vermin'll burn in hell for this."

Red looked back at Sarah. "Probably will, but won't be just for that, Missy." He chuckled and waved at the lookout up on top of a dark gray andesite outcrop.

"You're wastin' your time, there's no one to pay any ransom...my daddy's dead."

Moose glanced over at her. "Don't make no nevermind 'bout yer pa, girl...Got other plans fer you what don't require no ransom. Them what's young an' purty as you bring a right smart from the cat houses in the big cities...Ain't that a fact, Red?"

"What they say...Haw."

They rode into the slaver's camp beneath the old cliff dwellings. The two men dismounted as Sterling sauntered over.

"Mark her up?" He looked Sarah over as Red untied her hands and pulled her from the saddle.

"Said not to, didn't yuh?" asked Moose.

"That doesn't always seem to matter to you jaybirds." He grabbed Sarah's arm, spun her around and nodded. "She'll do. Get her up in the room."

Red took her from the boss as Moose walked over to the cliff wall, picked up the thirty foot ladder and leaned it against face, just below the lowest entrance.

"Climb." He nodded to her.

Sarah glared at him and started up the narrow ladder to the opening and crawled inside. She stood up, blinked several times waiting for her eyes to adjust to the dim light. Her nose wrinkled at the smell coming from the porcelain parlor pot.

"You'll get used to it," came a voice to her right.

Sarah could make out a number of figures, all sitting on blankets on the rock floor.

The nearest to her, the blonde, Sally Ann Loftin, pointed to a vacant blanket next to her. "Sit here."

Sarah sat down and could see the Navajo beside her.

"I'm Yellow Bird. Think you are the last."

Sarah frowned. "Last what?"

"We're being sold to bordellos an' parlor houses…We'll be girls of the line. You know, whores, prostitutes…sometimes called Fallen Angels."

"Oh, my God." She looked around trying to pierce the darkness. "Any way out?"

Sally shook her head. "Not without jumpin'."

"Meby not so," commented Yellow Bird.

Sarah glanced at her. "What do you mean?"

"These sky villages of the ancient ones always have back way out."

Sally got to her feet. "Where?"

BAR M RANCH

Bone stepped over and popped his sternum with the side of his fist, then started applying rhythmic pressure with his hands crossed in the center of his chest. "Loraine!"

She immediately put two fingers of her left hand behind Sky's jaw and pushed forward, pinched his nose with her right, then leaned over, covered his mouth with hers and exhaled.

Loraine synchronized her mouth-to-mouth following each of Bone's compression's at one per second.

She and Bone continued the CPR for almost two minutes when Gentle Sky coughed and took a breath on his own. Loraine held up her hand for Bone to stop.

Silke cocked her head. "How did ya'll know to do that?"

Loraine looked at her. "Uh…It's something we were…uh, trained to do as cops."

"Seen doctors do that breathin' thing in the cavalry but not pushin' on the chest before," said Tyree.

Bone shot a glance at Loraine. "One of our doctors back home had the idea to try it when a child was pulled out of the river not breathing and his heart wasn't beating…He figured pushin' on the outside of the kid's chest would squeeze the heart while someone else did the breathin'…It worked. Been doin' it ever since."

Silke nodded. "Huh? Makes sense." She looked down at Sky. "He's breathin', deeper than before."

"Might of had a clot or something," offered Bone.

The girls continued their ministrations. Silke got most of the blood cleaned away. Loraine took the wicker bottle of tequila and poured some in each wound.

Gentle Sky squirmed but didn't awaken.

Haven shook some of the alum powder from the vial into each bullet hole while Silke followed her with a dollop of wild honey. Loraine placed a thick pad made from a folded piece of towel over the individual entry wounds.

She looked to Bone and Tyree. "Need to turn him again so we can do the same to the back. It'll be all we can do till the doc gets here…Honey'll hold those pads on till we can bind them."

Haven grabbed Loraine's arm. "He stopped breathin' again!"

§§§

CHAPTER FOURTEEN

VALLES CALDERA

Sarah looked around the dimly lit, shadowy room. "Where do you think the escape hole might be?"

Yellow Bird glanced back at her. "Above head…on back wall."

"Do they bring food an' water in the evening?" asked Sarah.

Sally nodded. "Uh-huh...'fore sundown."

"Be about another thirty minutes then, I think...I would say let's wait till after they bring it an' leave before we go to lookin' for it."

"Why wait, Sarah?"

"They probably won't be back before mornin' so if we find somethin' we won't be interrupted, plus they won't know we've left...Right, Sally?"

"Oh, right. Didn't think about that."

"Yellow Bird, where do these escape holes usually lead to?"

"Most lead to top of cliff or back side through mountain."

Sarah looked around their small prison and could count ten other girls, eight Indian, one Mexican, and two white—Sally Ann and herself. She had found out that the Indian girls were Pueblo, Apache, and Navajo—all under sixteen.

The sun was settling below the mountains behind the cliff after one of the men brought a bucket of gruel, a bucket of water, and an empty parlor pot.

Sally glanced out of the front opening and could see most of the men gathered around the fire, drinking, and a light inside the Bubash and Sterling tent.

Sarah looked at Yellow Bird's shape in the semidarkness. "How do we find this hole?"

"Feel."

She stepped over to the left side corner of the back wall, raised up on her tiptoes and placed her hands high as she could over her head against the adobe surface.

Yellow Bird shuffled her moccasined feet to the right as she felt along the wall in the darkness. She only moved three feet before stopping.

"Here...Yellow Bird find."

Sarah moved closer to her. "How wide is it?"

"From fingers to elbow."

"Pretty small...about sixteen inches."

"Ancients small people. Can go through one at time...Hope not meet *Yee naaldooshii*."

"What's a *Yee naaldooshii*?"

"Skinwalker," came Yellow Bird's voice.

"Mean he who walk on all fours...evil spirit...witches," came another voice. "Me Moon

Water…Navajo…Skinwalkers can change to look like any creature…Much evil."

"Shapeshifters," muttered Sarah.

"Who goes first?" asked Sally Ann.

Sarah stepped close to the wall. "I will…Ya'll help me up an' each of us will help the next until we're all inside…We crawl out in single file."

BAR M RANCH

Bone quickly stepped over to perform CPR again as Loraine repeated her earlier action. It didn't take as long this time as before until the big man started breathing again.

Bone did not remove his hands, but kept them on Gentle Sky's chest, closed his eyes and dropped his head down.

A soft blue light seemed to emanate between his hands and Sky's chest as it slowly rose and fell. A knowing Loraine pulled a slatback chair up behind Bone's legs.

An almost imperceptible quiver ran through his body as the glow got brighter. It turned to a shake, after a moment the glow evaporated, then Bone collapsed into the chair. Loraine held it to keep him from tilting back over. Silke and Haven stepped to each side so he wouldn't topple out.

Tyree frowned. "What just happened?"

Luz glanced at him. "Bone knows how to do the layin' on of hands thing. You know, like in the Bible." She looked at Berkley. "Did it to you, too, when you were unconscious."

"I didn't know."

Loraine smiled at him. "No way you could have…He doesn't talk about it, just does it when it's necessary…It's very exhaustin' for him."

Berkley shook his head. "My, my."

Luz left the room and quickly returned with a quart Mason jar of water as Bone shook his head, blinked several times, looked around, then down at the chair he was sitting in. "Thanks, Babe."

"How'd he know it was her?" asked Tyree.

"They've been together for a number of years," answered Haven.

Luz handed him the jar, which he promptly turned it up, drained it and handed it back. "More, please."

Tyree looked puzzled.

Haven leaned close to him. "He has to have a lot of water when he does that...Don't know why."

Tyree nodded, but still looked confused. "Ah...Think there's a lot 'bout these folks I don't know."

Two hours later, Pablo appeared in the doorway with the doctor behind him. "*Señora*, I bring Doctor Owens."

He moved aside as the forty something doctor with salt and pepper hair from Santa Fe, Doctor Andrew Owens, stepped quickly into the room with his black leather bag.

"I need everyone out but two ladies to assist me...Good God, he's a big one, isn't he? That will work in his favor."

"My cousin an' I will help, Doc...I'm Silke, she's Haven."

He looked first at one, then the other. "I would have figured you to be sisters."

Haven nodded. "Get that a lot."

He walked over to the wash basin, removed his coat, rolled up his sleeves and started washing his hands using the bar of lye soap lying beside it.

Silke handed him a clean towel.

"You've done this before?"

She nodded. "Yes, sir."

Luz led everyone else from the room. "Anybody for coffee?"

Bone grinned. "Thought you'd never bring it up, Luz."

Doctor Owens dried his hands and forearms, stepped over to Gentle Sky, placed his stethoscope on his chest on top of the bandages and listened for a moment. "Lungs clear...Surprisingly he has a strong heartbeat with, what? Four gunshot wounds?"

Silke nodded. "Three through and through and one's still in there."

"Remove the bandages, please." He set what supplies he thought he might need, including a small metal tray with a scalpel, forceps and probe on the night stand. "May have to set up an office out here, this keeps up...Looked like Mister Berkley was doing well."

Haven pulled up the large lard bucket. She and Silke could use the trash container for the partially blood-soiled bandages. "Yes, sir, this was the first day he's been out of bed."

"Quick healer."

He leaned over to inspect the wounds after the girls had pulled the last of the bandages out from under Sky's body.

Doctor Owens noticed the quart jar of honey on the dresser. "Figured ya'll'd use that combination of tequila, powdered alum and honey again like on Mister Berkley."

Silke grinned. "Ain't broke, don't fix it."

"Have to agree with that." He felt of Sky's pulse. "Glad he's still out...Hand me that probe, please."

Haven picked up the long metal rod and handed it to him.

"Without rolling him over just yet, which of the bullet holes wasn't a pass through?"

"That lower right one, Doc," said Silke.

He nodded, gently spread the skin and slowly inserted the ten inch probe in the wound. The trajectory required him to slightly angle to the right and up as he eased the rod deeper.

"Ah, found the little scudder...Those long straight forceps, please." He held out his hand without looking as Haven laid the surgical tool in his palm.

Holding the probe with his left, he inserted the forceps and followed the rod down to the slug. He spread the finger holes slightly apart, then closed and latched them while he pulled the probe out.

"Now, the *coup de grace*." Doctor Owens slowly backed the locked forceps from the deep wound. "*Voilà*." He held the bloody misshapened lump of lead up to the light coming from the window, studied it for a moment, then nodded. "All in one piece...A .45 I'd say...It was flattened against the back side of his scapula...shoulder blade, if you will."

Silke cleaned the blood from the wound. "Should I pour a little tequila in it, Doctor?"

He nodded. "Then sprinkle a goodly portion of that alum powder...we'll give it a minute or so to constrict the capillaries and stop the bleeding, then pack it with that honey."

"Is that honey thing something new, Doc?" asked Haven.

He laughed. "Goodness no, my dear, it was used on wounds as far back as the Romans. The Centurions always carried a good supply of honey when they went into battle...Best I can find out, the Father of medicine, Hippocrates himself, suggested it far back as 400 BC. Nothing better than honey to prevent corruption."

He looked into the wound. "Go ahead and add it now."

VALLES CALDERA

Sarah crawled on her hands and knees through the stygian darkness. Yellow Bird was directly behind her touching the bottom of her feet as they moved along.

Abruptly the smallness of the tunnel changed to an open area. Sarah slowly got to her feet, felt over head and found only empty space. She reached to the right and could feel the rough texture of the wall as opposed to the smoothness of the adobe.

If there were light, she would realize they had entered an lava tube from the ancient collapsed volcano. The Anasazi Indians who had built the outlying pueblo had walled the lava tube at the caldera where they built the cliff dwelling into a ventilation shaft as well as an emergency escape route.

She turned and assisted each girl to her feet as they emerged from the adobe tube into the lava chamber.

"We can walk from here…I think. Let's stay in single file, holding on to the shoulder of the person in front of you an' keep your other hand against the side wall."

"I feel a breeze," said Sally Ann. "From our backs."

"Must lead to the outside," offered Sarah.

They started moving slowly forward with Sarah still leading the way. She suddenly stopped.

"Why do you stop?" asked Yellow Bird.

"Heard a noise…There's someone or something in here with us."

§§§

CHAPTER FIFTEEN

BAR M RANCH

The sun had set behind the mountains when Doctor Owens straightened up as he tied off the final wrap of the torn sheet strips around Gentle Sky's broad chest. "That should do it…Now we wait."

Silke handed him a clean towel. "Bet Martina's got supper on."

The doctor grinned and dabbed his brow with the towel. "Best thing I've heard today." He gave a final glance at Sky's chest slowly rising and falling. "Looks stable. We'll check on him every ten minutes or so." He nodded to the doorway. "Shall we?"

Gentle Sky moaned softly. They turned to look at him and saw his eyes flutter, and then open with a temporary look of confusion.

Owens stepped back to the bed. "How do you feel?"

"Water," he wheezed.

Silke picked up a half-full pint Mason jar, lifted Sky's head and held it to his lips. "Slow."

He blinked his understanding and drank several swallows before nodding and looking up in Silke's face. "Bone."

She turned to Haven who immediately left the room.

In a few seconds, she came back in followed by Bone, Loraine, and Tyree.

Sky turned his deep brown eyes up at Bone as he leaned over and placed his hand on the Indian's forearm. "Find Sarah." His eyes showed the depth of his request.

Bone nodded. "Leaving at first light."

Sky struggled to rise. "*Enah Mahah*, go."

Bone moved his hand up to his shoulder to ease him back down. "Don't think so, friend. You must heal…Rest now."

The Indian pursed his lips and nodded slightly, but stared at Bone, his eyes pleading.

"We'll find her…trust me on that. They can run but they can't hide."

Sky nodded and closed his eyes.

The group walked back to the big dining room and took seats around the long plank trestle table.

Martina moved around the diners filling their wine glasses. She had already placed platters of beef enchiladas, rice, and refried beans at each chair.

Doctor Owens picked up his glass of port, took a sip, set the long stemmed goblet back on the table, and shook his head. "For the life of me I don't understand how that big man is still alive. By all rights, considering how much blood he lost alone…he should have been dead long before I got here."

Bone glanced across the table. "There's something to be said about will, Doc. Got a sayin' back home…called the power of positive thinking."

Owens put a forkfull of the thick enchilada covered in chili sauce in his mouth and chewed. He looked at Martina still filling glasses. "These are wonderful."

"*Gracias, Señor*…I make *Señor* Bone's favorite desert, also…peach cobbler."

Bone grinned at her. "Could smell it when we walked in here, Martina…Nothin' in the world smells like hot peach cobbler."

The doctor looked back at Bone. "I would have to agree you're correct about Gentle Sky. His will power is the key. Sky's concern for his young charge is overriding what his body has gone through…Still, all in all, he's not out of the woods, yet."

Silke looked up from her plate. "Don't think there's any question that's what's keepin' him goin'."

Haven glanced at her cousin. "Just hope we don't disappoint him."

Bone's gold-flecked eyes flashed. "Not in this lifetime."

VALLES CALDERA

"Don't hear anything now, Sarah…You?"

"No, Sally." She tried to peer into the darkness. "Let's go on an' follow the breeze."

"Me see light."

"Oh, my, you're right, Yellow Bird…Stars."

Several of the girls behind sobbed softly.

"*Usen* is kind," whispered Sweet Water, one of the Apaches, as they moved forward.

Sarah stepped out into a clear, cool, moonless night. There was a ledge almost three feet wide in front of the lava tube. The ancient weathered flow extended down the hill.

The ledge had apparently been carved out of the hardened black basalt by the Neolithic inhabitants of the area and led downhill at an angle to the wooded swale with a running stream, over two hundred feet below.

The eleven girls gathered at the mouth of the cave and on the ledge for a few moments, thanking their God and breathing of the unfettered pure mountain air.

They moved slowly again, single file, down the narrow trail as it zigzagged down the incline to where the piñon, cedar, and aspen began and the trail widened. The starlit night was a vast improvement over the pitch-blackness of the cave.

Sally walked up beside Sarah. "Wonder what that noise was back in the cave?"

"Don't know an' don't think I want to know…Smelled like something dead, too."

"I know."

Yellow Bird walked up beside them. "Meby it *Pukwudgie*."

Sally turned to the Navajo. "What's a *Pukwudgie*?"

"Sometime kind *Yee naaldooshii*, Skinwalker…Small." She held her hand below her waist. "This big. They sometime help, but sometime be trickster, like coyote…sometime kill…Live in dark places like cave."

"Well, they or it, let us pass."

Sarah led the exhausted group up to the gurgling stream.

Sally touched her arm. "Do you think we can stop and rest awhile?"

Sarah looked around and could make out a grassy patch near the stream. "Good idea, Sally, we can rest here next to the water. Don't know about you, but I'm thirsty."

"Me too."

Sarah turned to the others. "Let's rest here till daylight. That all right with ya'll?"

There were several mutterings of approval from the girls as they found a place to lie down.

Sunlight filtered through the leaves of the overhead branches as a mockingbird ran through his repertoire of songs and was joined by a pair of cardinals.

The girls were all bunched together in an effort to keep warm as they slept in the cool of early morning.

Sarah's eyes were the first to open and they focused on a tall, lean, gray-haired man. He was dressed in a dark brown wool vest over a boiled cotton shirt, red kerchief around his neck, canvas pants, and a weathered gray Stetson. There was a five pointed star pinned to his vest.

She jumped erect with a gasp.

"It's all right, young lady, I'm Sheriff Russell. Been lookin' for ya'll…Everone all right?"

Sarah glanced around at the other girls, then back to the lawman as she got to her feet and nodded. "How did you find us?"

He smiled, showing his even white teeth. "Pure luck…or God's will. I…"

The sheriff was interrupted by a distant, muted scream from up the mountain and two muffled gunshots.

He and the girls looked up through the trees in the direction of the cave.

"Hmm, must be somethin' in that cave…I suggest we should get away from here while we can…Follow me." He turned and headed along the game trail, downstream, following the bubbling waterway.

"You don't have a posse or anything?" asked Sally Ann.

He shook his head. "Know this country like the back of my hand, Missy. Posse just slow me down."

They walked through the woods for almost a mile until they came to a larger trail that crossed the stream.

"Ya'll wait here, I need to go find a wagon or some horses for you...Never be able to walk out of here. My horse is just up the way a bit...May take several hours...Just stay put."

He waded across the stream and headed west along the wider trail until he disappeared.

SANTA FE FOREST

Tyree led Bone, Loraine, Silke, and Haven along the trail through the thick woods.

Bear Dog padded beside *Lakná*, Silke's dun, stopping occasionally to water a bush or smell some coon scat.

Bone trailed Ted, their pack mule, as they worked up the incline of the outer lip of the Valles Caldera on the east side.

Fox squirrels chattered and fussed at the group as they passed through the tree rodents domain. A redheaded woodpecker hammered a tattoo on a Douglas fir in search of breakfast.

Silke focused on the tracks they were following as Haven rode alongside Tyree's grula. Her Cheyenne war bow was in a scabbard on *d'Artagnan's* left side with the quiver of arrows on top of it, hung from a saddle string. Haven's Winchester .45-70 rifle was on the right in it's boot.

"No question, these are the prints of Sarah's paint. Recognize 'em from back at the house."

"How do you do that, cuz?"

Silke glanced back at Haven. "My mentor, Chickasaw Lighthorse Red Wolf, taught me that hoof prints are just like people's faces...all different. It's a matter of finding a certain point or spot in the print...Might be the shape of this particular horse's frog or a chip or dent in a shoe."

"My gut tells me they're headed to the west side of the caldera...There are several cliff dwellin's along there," said Tyree.

"Let's do what Bass Reeves always said, then."

"What's that, Bone?"

"He said, 'Don't track 'em, jest go where they be goin' an' meet 'em there...Gots to think like one of them miscreants'."

"Sounds good to me." Tyree bumped his horse into a single foot trot.

VALLES CALDERA

"Well, looky, looky…What do we have here?"

Tater Adams glanced at Ollie Wilkes beside him.

"Look like some lost angels, I'd say, Tater."

Three Owls, Coon Creede, Jess Shepherd and Shadow Butler joined Adams and Wilkes as they stepped out of the woods in a semicircle around the girls—all had smirks on their face.

Sally Ann screamed as she backed up against Sarah…

§§§

CHAPTER SIXTEEN

VALLES CALDERA

The intrepid group topped the hogback at the southeastern edge of the caldera. They surveyed the picturesque panoramic scene of the fourteen mile wide bowl beneath them. The serene bucolic nature of the environment belied the violence of the massive volcano that existed here over a million years ago.

Tyree crossed his hands on top of his saddlehorn and leaned forward, creating a little space between his rear and the cantle of his saddle. He studied the hazy sky overhead, focused his view on the western horizon on the other side of the caldera, then rubbed the back of his neck vigorously.

Haven glanced at him. "What's the matter, Tyree?"

He shook his head and looked back at her, then at the others. "Lived in this country too long. Skin itches."

Silke looked up from perusing the tracks. "And?"

"Look at the western sky."

"Alright...So?" asked Haven.

"See anything?"

She shook her head. "Like the rest of the sky...hazy."

"There's a very slight red tinge to it down low...See now?"

Haven frowned. "I'll bite."

He pinched his lips below his full dark mustache. "Sand storm comin'…My skin always itches. Gonna be a Jim Bob bangup one, I'm thinkin'."

Bone eased up beside them. "That's bad, I take it?"

"Is…Scour the hide right off yer face an' the paint off a board…Gotta find some shelter fer us an the animals." He looked at the horizon again. "Gonna be here by sundown."

Loraine looked over at him. "Any suggestions?"

He nodded. "Meby…Gotta go back a ways. Need to git away from the west face of this ridge, start with. Believe there's some caves off to the north an' below us a ways."

Bone arched an eyebrow. "What's 'a ways'?"

Silke grinned. "'Bout the same as 'yonder', Bone."

"Oh, shoulda said so…Lead on McGruff."

"Think it's 'Lay on Macduff', from Shakespeare's *Macbeth*," corrected Haven.

Bone's grin was a little sideways. "Close enough." He turned Hildebrandt in trail to Tyree's Laddie as they headed back down the slope angling to the left.

Tyree led their way across the eastern slope at a greater angle down and back into the tree line.

He pointed. "See that thrust up there?"

Everyone nodded. "The only caves in this caldera are old, what they call, 'lava tubes'…where molten rock poured out of the side of the volcano…Left a lot of 'em 'round here. Some deep…Some not so."

"Well, leastwise, the storm will be blastin' the other side," said Silke.

Tyree nodded. "That's the point…The deeper, the better, though. That wind will be acurlin' over the top an' whippin' back…He raised his head and sniffed. "Smell that?…Dust…Like smellin' rain 'fore it comes."

"What's that over there?" Haven pointed at a dark area behind a copse of shaky aspen several hundred yards across the face of the ridge.

Tyree nodded. "Could be. Let's check it out."

Bear Dog loped on ahead of the group, stopped at the grove of aspen, turned and woo-wooed at Silke.

"Think he's sayin' it's a cave."

"How kin you tell," asked Tyree.

She smiled. "I listen."

They trotted diagonally across the incline, dropping down another hundred feet until they reached the aspens.

Tyree dismounted, ground-tied his gelding, and walked up to the opening. There were several thirty-foot ponderosa pines to the right of the opening. He looked up a little ways and broke a dead limb the size of his wrist from the trunk.

Taking a Lucifer from his vest, he lit it with his thumb nail and held the hissing, sputtering, yellow flame against the butt of the limb where the most concentrated pitch was. The highly flammable pine sap popped, sizzled, and burst into a flame that slowly crept around until the entire end of the branch was burning.

Bear Dog entered the dark opening. He was followed by Tyree who cleared the spider webs from across the cavity with the burning torch, stepped into the cavern, and disappeared in short order—except for the flickering flame.

Tyree stepped back out, leaned the torch against the outer edge of the basalt as Bear Dog came back from the depths of the tunnel, occasionally glancing behind him and whining low.

"What is it, boy?" Tyree ruffled his fur in back of his ears. "See boogers or just find some old lion scat?"

The half wolf sat down and looked up at him, and then over at Silke.

"Somethin' in there he doesn't like, but he's not pitchin' a real fit over it."

Tyree walked over to the ponderosa pines. "Be a good idea to break off a couple more of these dead limbs for torches, plus gather some firewood."

Loraine scooped up some dry pine needles and loose bark for kindling. "Ya'll get some limbs and I'll get a fire started inside…after we take care of the stock, that is."

Bone, Haven, and Silke led the horses and Ted down slope to a nearby stream and let them drink their fill.

Tyree gathered some more of the pine knots and carried them to the opening. He picked up the still burning first one and led Silke and the others with the animals deeper in the cave where they could strip their tack.

Over fourteen miles away on the far side of the caldera the gang members sent to round up the girls led them over the top of the ridge and back down to the cliff dwellings. The western sky was already showing a massive red wall of dust reaching up into the stratosphere, boiling and churning as it rolled to the east.

They made it into the camp and hustled the girls back up the ladder to their prison.

"Grover Red, you got first watch inside their room," said Sterling.

"Why me?"

"Because I said so…'Nybody know what happened to Hardy? He was followin' 'em through the cave."

"Him no come out," said Three Owls. "Hear shots…Mebe *Yee naaldlooshii* no like."

"What's *Yee naaldlooshii*?"

"Skinwalker, evil spirit."

"Hogwash."

Three Owls' ebony eyes glared at Sterling. "Him no here."

An hour later, a massive red wall of dust blocked out the setting sun. The wind was already whipping over the top of the ridge above the cave entrance.

Loraine had a fire going inside near the mouth, with the coffee pot on. She looked up as a shadow crossed the opening—Sheriff Case Russell was leading his horse up to the entrance.

"Hello the cave."

"Come on in, Sheriff. Room in the back for your horse with ours...Coffee's on."

Tyree walked out and took the reins to the sheriff's mount. "I'll strip him down for you, Sheriff, go ahead and have some coffee."

"'Preciate it, Tyree." He stopped at the fire as Loraine handed him a steaming cup.

"Looks like you made it just in time, Case."

He nodded to Loraine and squatted down. "I'd say. Cut it fair close, though."

Bone chuckled. "Close only counts in horseshoes and hand grenades."

Russell laughed. "Haven't heard that before."

"What are you doin' out here?" asked Silke.

"Lookin' for those girls...Purty familiar with this area. Figured might run into ya'll."

Haven looked at him. "Any luck?"

He nodded and took a sip. "Found 'em."

Everyone looked up."

"Where?" asked Bone.

"On the other side of the caldera. They had escaped out the back of the cliff dwellin' ruins they were bein' held in...through a lava tube like this'un. I hid 'em out while I was ridin' to git a wagon...Then this storm come up." He took another sip of his coffee.

Silke pursed her lips. "Hope they found some shelter."

"'Magine they did. 'Bout nine of 'em were Injun...Know to git outta that wind."

"How many all together are there?" asked Haven.

"Counted eleven, two white."

Bone poured himself a little more coffee. "That cornsilk hair girl...name's Sarah...She amongst them?"

He nodded. "She's the one what led 'em out through the back of the mountain...Smart girl, gutsy too."

They all looked out the front at the tree tops bending from the force of the howling wind in the eerie red murk.

"Good thing we got ourselves an' our stock in this here cave. This kinda storm been known to kill a body," said Tyree. "Dust can git so thick, easy to suffocate in it."

"How long do you think it'll last, Tyree," asked Haven.

He shook his head. "No tellin'. Sometimes few hours, sometimes...couple days."

Bone frowned. "Joy."

The horses in the back stomped their feet nervously and snorted loudly.

Bear Dog got to his feet and faced the rear of the cave. The hackles along his back stood erect as a growl rumbled deep in his throat, then turned to a whine...

§§§

CHAPTER SEVENTEEN

VALLES CALDERA

The very walls inside the pueblo cliff dwelling seemed to shake with the buffeting of the vicious wind outside. Dust drifted down from the ceiling.

Glover Red sat with his back against the wall below the vent the girls had escaped through. Eerie deep shadows were cast about the room from a coal-oil lantern, its wick low, burning next to his feet.

The three ringleaders of the attempted escape, Sarah, Sally Ann, and Yellow Bird were in the far corner huddled together in the darkness.

"Now what do we do?" whispered Sally.

"Wait till white eyes fall asleep, kill and go out small tunnel again," said Yellow Bird.

"We don't have anything to kill him with...They removed all the rocks and sticks before we were put in here."

"Sarah's right. And we're not strong enough to overpower him before he cried out...or even choke him in his sleep."

Only the whites of Yellow Bird's dark eyes showed in the dim light from the lantern. "*Usen* will provide...Mebe send *Diyin Diné'e*, the Holy People to work blessing."

"What do you mean?" asked Sally Ann.

"*Diyin Diné'e* sometime use the evil Skinwalker as messenger."

Sarah frowned in the darkness. "But how?"

"Not good to talk about Skinwalkers...they no like."

Glover Red's head bobbed several times, sank to his chest, jerked back up, sank again—and then stayed. The wind outside continued to howl, drowning his snores.

The buffeting of the storm diminished to a steady white noise roar for the night. Everyone in the pueblo and the rest of the men in the gang ensconced in some of the other dwellings all slept.

Silke took a sip of her coffee and glanced at Tyree. "What do you think that was back in the tunnel what had the animals spooked?"

"Well, fer starters, Miss Silke, I'd say not'n my department...but since yer wantin' to know, my guess'd be most logically a armadilla."

"An' not most logically?"

Tyree glanced a little apprehensively at the blackness in the back of the tunnel, back at Silke, and then to Haven. Everyone else was rolled up in their blankets for the night.

"This here is Navajo country, as I'm sure ya'll know. The Navajos are very religious as well as a superstitious people. Their ancestors...leastwise the folks what come before them, were called the Ancient Ones…"

"Oh, the *Anasazi*," interrupted Haven. "They built a big city of pueblos at a place called Chaco Canyon here in New Mexico."

"Yessum. That's them…Chaco Canyon is due east of here, a little ways."

Silke stirred the fire sending a shower of sparks swirling up above the ring of rocks. "Didn't they kinda disappear before the Spaniards came through this country in the 1500s?"

"Did that, too…Seems they had a lot of spiritual beliefs includin' believin' they could go to other worlds through certain doorways er windows called portals. They called it the Fourth World…"

"They just all of a sudden seemed to vanish somewhere in the 1300s…All of 'em, didn't they?"

Tyree nodded. "What the Navajo believe, Haven…Anyhoo, they also believed in spirits…evil ones an' good ones. You know, Skinwalkers an' Shapeshifters?"

Haven put her hand to her mouth. "Oh, my."

"These spirits could take on the shape of any creature…'cludin' other people."

"Other people?" gasped Silke.

"Uh-huh...Now, the Navajo won't hardly talk 'bout 'em for fear of re...ret..."

"Retribution?"

"Close enough, Haven...But, they'll swear an' be damned these Skinwalkers live in dark places, can go back an' forth 'tween worlds, an' can be bad or good...they's no way of knowin'...Sometimes they take folks with 'em, never to be seen er heard from ag'in."

Silke looked over the top of her cup. "You're sayin' there's a Skinwalker back in the bowels of this mountain in these lava tubes?"

He rubbed the stubble on his chin. "Well, ain't sayin' there is, an' ain't sayin' there ain't...Just sayin' what the Navajo believe. Known a goodly number of Navajo Shaman...Not somebody you want to get on the bad side of."

Silke and Haven both looked into the pitch blackness behind them.

Silke tossed the dregs from her cup in the fire where it sizzled on a burning limb. "Whatever...There's *somethin'* back there that Bear Dog is afraid of an' I've never seen him afraid of anything...man or beast."

BAR M RANCH

The wind had died down substantially but there was still a great deal of dust swirling about in the air.

Elizabeth brought a tray with a steaming mug of herbal tea for Gentle Sky. "Like some tea, Mister Sky?"

His dark brown eyes took in the blue-eyed child in the dim light cast by the single coal oil lantern and he nodded. "Uhh...good."

His head was propped up on several pillows, Elizabeth had brushed and braided his long hair into two thick braids, tied at the end with thin strips of latigo.

She held the cup to his lips so he could sip Martina's special arrowroot, milkweed, and willow bark tea for pain and to ease breathing.

"Uhh." He nodded enough for the moment.

Luz entered the room followed by Reg using a cane.

"Are we feelin' better Gentle Sky?" She laid her palm on his forehead.

"Uhh, me better."

"Martina's makin' you some fresh bone broth. Good for you considerin' all the blood you lost."

"I can attest to that, Gentle Sky. Fed it to me till I was up on my feet," said Berkley. "Of course it was not like I had much of a choice." He smiled.

Sky looked up at him, then at Luz and nodded. "No word from Bone?"

She shook her head. "Not yet. Won't know nothin' till they get back."

"Must stop them…End evil…Make pay."

"I'm sure they will. Not much quit in Bone or any of 'em."

"Uhh, me know…Sarah need help."

She patted his shoulder. "Not to worry, Gentle Sky. They'll find 'er."

He sighed, fluttered his eye lids several times, and drifted off.

"Take the tea back to Martina, Lizbeth, she'll keep it warm."

Elizabeth looked over at the sleeping Indian. "He's sure worried about her…said her father was not a good man."

Luz nodded. "Can vouchsafe that."

VALLES CALDERA

The storm had dropped to just a moderately strong wind but was still full of sand and dust. Bubash climbed the ladder to the cliff dwelling room where the gang was hunkered down and stepped inside the small doorway.

He looked around at the men. "Three Owls, you go relieve Grover Red with the girls."

The Apache raised his head from atop his drawn up knees and looked stoically at Bubash. "Three Owls no go room with tunnel…Send someone else."

"I said you go, redhide."

"No."

"What's the matter, Injun, you scared?"

Three Owls rose slowly to his feet. "No man may call *Tai' Múh* coward and live…Especially no *pindah-lickyoee*." He placed his hand on the war tomahawk at his belt.

Even in the pale light, it was obvious that Marvin Bubash's skin blanched. He abruptly turned to another of the men. "Uh…It's Welch's turn anyway. Go relieve him, Moose."

"Shore, Boss." The rail thin man got to his feet, adjusted his gunbelt and donned his battered felt hat.

Bubash glanced briefly at Three Owls, who had not moved from where he stood, turned and followed Welch out the doorway and back down the ladder.

The two men lowered their heads against the wind and made their way down to the ladder lying on the ground below the girl's room.

Bubash stood beside the ladder as Welch picked it up and propped it against the wall underneath the small doorway—he climbed up and entered.

Bubash waited a moment for Grover Red to come out before continuing on to the next room where he and Sterling had taken refuge during the storm from their tent.

It was Moose who stuck his head back out the entry. "Hey, Boss, Red ain't in here."

"What? What are you sayin' man?…Where is he?"

"Don't know. Just ain't here…The gals is, but he's not."

"Dammit to hell," exclaimed Bubash as he started to climb the ladder.

Rudolph Sterling stuck his head out of his doorway as did a couple of the men from the gang's room.

"What is it, Bubash?" asked Sterling.

"Moose says Grover Red's gone," he answered from halfway up the ladder.

"The hell you say...He run off on us?"

"How should I know?...Just ain't there."

Bubash entered the room as Sterling strode out of his doorway, over to the ladder and started to climb.

He reached the top, entered and looked around the room as Bubash turned the lantern up to cast more light.

The girls were all sitting up from their blankets and rubbing the sand from their eyes.

Bubash pointed at a crumpled blanket against the wall. "Here's where he sat."

Sterling looked at Sarah. "Where'd he go?"

She glanced at Sally and Yellow Bird and shook her head. "He was there durin' the storm...before we all fell asleep."

Sterling bent over and picked up Grover Red's old dark green bowler.

Bubash looked at it, and then up at the dark hole that led to the tunnel. "He don't go nowhere without that hat."

He and Sterling exchanged glances.

Yellow Bird smiled surreptitiously in the shadows.

§§§

CHAPTER EIGHTEEN

VALLES CALDERA

The morning in New Mexico broke bright, clear, and cool. All signs of the storm had moved to the east except for a coating of sand and dust on everything, including the leaves on the trees outside.

Loraine had a small fire going, the coffee pot was on, and bacon sizzled in a pan filling the confines of the cave with the tantalizing odors.

Sheriff Russell walked over from his bedroll, rubbing his face with both hands. "Mornin', Loraine, smells good…Coffee ready?"

She smiled at him. "It is. Help yourself."

He picked up the tin cup he had left close to the fire pit last night, used his kerchief to grab the hot pot handle, and filled it.

"What are your plans, Sheriff?"

"Reckon I'd best go on an' find a wagon. Only way we're gonna get the girls back to Santa Fe."

Silke had walked up while he was pouring his coffee. "Believe that would be a good idea…You say you left the girls on the west side of the caldera?"

"Did…On the back side of the ridge where the old cliff-dwellin's are."

"I know where those old ruins be," said Tyree as he came into the cave from outside after taking care of his morning ablutions. He squatted down and filled his cup also.

"Be quicker to skirt the south edge of the caldera rather than cross, and then climb the ridge to git to the other side…Pretty rough goin'."

Tyree nodded. "Good point, Sheriff…Right 'bout bein' rough goin'…Hard on horseflesh."

Bone and Haven were the last to arrive at the cook fire. Loraine handed him his coffee, the way he liked it—black.

"About time you got up."

"For your information I was up before sunup checking on things, short-stuff…You were still cuttin' logs. Snorin' like a freight train."

Loraine swatted him across his wide chest, causing him to spill some of his coffee. "Damn you, Bone, I do not!"

He giggled and blew across the top of his cup before he took a sip.

Haven looked at the pair and grinned. "How do ya'll keep from killin' each other?"

Loraine winked at her. "He's afraid of me…and I'm glad of it."

Marvin Bubash an' Rudolph Sterling had moved back out to their tent since the storm passed.

Sterling picked up his coffee cup and took a sip. "Men are gettin' kinda shook up over Grover Red and Hardy's disappearance. They're buyin' that horse crap Three Owls is spreadin' 'bout Skinwalkers an' Shapeshifters...Boogermen, haints, haw!"

Bubash looked at him from his camp chair. "When do those additional men get here?"

"This afternoon...accordin' to the man."

"What? Five?"

"Yep, what he said. We'll need 'em when we transport the merchandise."

"Let's send them plus the half-breed an' that trouble-makin' 'Pache out to take care of that bunch with the Pinkertons that are on our tail."

Sterling nodded and took another sip. "I can go with that. Don't need anymore flies in the buttermilk."

"Where do you think they'll be when them gunhawks get here?"

"Less I miss my guess, should be 'bout on the southern edge of the rim."

Bubash nodded. "Be a good place for an ambush."

"Three more days an' we're done with this batch."

"If we can keep the men settled down that long."

"Money is a great motivator."

"Mayhaps we should offer a bonus…say like a night in one of those brothels we'll be dealin' with?"

Bubash nodded again. "Think some of the men been eyein' one or two of them gals anyway."

Sterling grinned. "As have I, friend, as have I."

"Me too…'specially that little fourteen year old white girl, Sally something or other. Like to try me some of that."

"You'll have your chance." Bubash's upper lip curled up in a cross between a sneer and a malevolent smile.

Silke threw her saddle on *Lakná's* back on top of her saddle blanket. She reached under the front and lifted a bubble in the blanket up into the gullet, threaded the latigo in the cinch O ring, and pulled it up.

Haven watched her as she, too, slung her saddle atop *d'Artagnan*. "What do you, Tyree, Bone, an' Loraine all do that for, cuz?"

She looked at Haven on the other side from her gelding, her brow furrowed. "Do what?"

"Lift the blanket up in the gullet like that?"

"Oh…somethin' I learned from Bass Reeves. If you leave the blanket flat and suck the saddle down on it when you chinch up, you can cause pressure points an' galls on each side of the whithers…if you're in the saddle all day."

"Really?"

Tyree looked up from tightening his cinch. "Plus it puts too much pressure on their spine which can make 'em cranky…You'll wonder why they put your butt in the dirt later in the day."

"Ah, that's why there's that open space underneath the saddle in the middle with the sheepskin on each side…Keeps the pressure off their back."

"Which you kill when you don't pull that bubble in your blanket," said Silke.

Haven nodded. "Good to know."

Tyree grinned. "'Specially since we're gonna be in the saddle most of the day...Kinda like on a cattle drive."

Sheriff Russell waved back as he trotted off. "See ya'll when I get back with the wagon."

"How you going to find us?"

"Oh, never fear, Loraine, I'll find ya'll...This is my country."

They mounted and followed Tyree off to the southwest, skirting the rim through the pines and aspen as the Sheriff suggested, headed to the west side of the caldera. Bear Dog loped out ahead of them.

"Sure glad he found those girls, save us a lot of time," said Loraine.

Bone glanced over at his wife. "Just hope they're still all right where he left them."

"You mean from the storm?" chimed in Silke.

Bone paused for a long moment. "You don't really think the kidnappers are just goin' to be sitting around on their thumbs with their meal ticket on the loose, do you?"

A worried look came over Silke's face. "Oh, see what you mean."

Tyree bumped his grula up into a road trot. "Need to hurry every chance we get, put it that way."

Ten miles away on the north side of the caldera, the five hardened gunmen trotted their horses south across the middle of the big crater.

"How'd you manage to talk the man into payin' us half our money up front, Big Slim?"

The leader, a large man with one white eye in the middle of a long knife scar that ran from his forehead to the corner of his mouth, looked over at his number two, Hank Higgins, and chuckled. "Could tell he wuz 'gainst a rock an' a hard place so I said half or no deal."

"Half of a thousand per man in advance ain't chicken feed."

Big Slim Bonner set his jaw. "What I didn't tell him was we'd a done it fer nothin'."

"Nothin'?…What do you mean?"

"'Member me tellin' ya'll 'bout Marshal Lindsey's posse an' a couple of Pinkertons takin' out my brother Bull an' the rest of the

Bonner-Crossfield gang up in Apache City, Colorado, two weeks ago?"

"Yeah, kilt the lot of 'em…What was it, nine?" asked Hank.

Bonner nodded. "Nine, 'cludin' my brother Bull…Well, them two Pinkertons, Silke an' Haven Justice is leadin' this bunch we're gonna hit."

"Sounds like women names."

"Are."

"Women? They's women Pinks?"

"There are, an' these two is plumb salty, hear tell."

"Lordy, Lordy, ain't never kilt no woman law 'fore…Private er otherwise."

"Gonna git yer chanct, numb-nuts. Wuz tol'…no survivors."

"Reckon we gonna git a opportunity to have a little fun 'fore we skin 'em an' hang 'em?"

Big Slim glanced over at the tall hatchet-faced killer and grinned. "How'd you know?"

§§§

CHAPTER NINETEEN

VALLES CALDERA

The sun was almost at apogee overhead as Tyree led the group along the game trail to the west. The narrow path was covered with a low canopy of spruce, fir, cedar, and dogwood limbs causing them to do a lot of ducking and dodging as they slowed their mounts to a walk.

Bear Dog disappeared for five to ten minutes at a time but then would show back up—once with a woodchuck in his jaws. He laid down in the trail after everyone had passed to enjoy his lunchtime repast.

The trail meandered up and down the slope of the caldera rim, going around basalt thrusts and lava outflows long since cooled and hardened.

Haven nudged her gelding up beside Tyree. "Why don't we ride across those old lava flows...would seem to be shorter."

"Well, main reason while that lava looks solid...ain't necessarily so."

"What do you mean?"

"There's a lot of bubbles in there...some ten or twelve feet across an' sometimes twenty-thirty feet deep. The top is like a sheet of glass...can't tell till yer right on top an' yer horse breaks through...Down you go."

"Really? You're not funnin' me, are you?"

Tyree shook his head. "Uh-uh...The fall don't kill you, you'll be trapped in that hole, most likely with a broke-leg horse...Never see a wild horse or burro cross 'ny of that stuff...They stay away from it."

"Go to school on the wild creatures, huh, Tyree?"

"Purty much, Bone, purty much…Have to in this country."

Big Slim Bonner and his gang trotted their horses up the box canyon through the cedar and piñon pine and reined up at the camp in front of the cliff dwellings. They had been passed by the guard at the opening of the canyon.

Bubash and Sterling stepped away from their tent and over to the five gunhawks.

"Get down, boys, get down. Made good time," Sterling stuck his hand out to Big Slim. "Grab some coffee an' got some beans an' tortillas at the fire."

The barrel-chested man dismounted and shook the proffered hand. "Coffee sounds good." He glanced around. "Nice setup you got here. Glad we had good directions…woulda never found it."

Bubash smiled slightly. "That's the point."

"Ya'll rest a bit, water your horses…then got a little chore for you."

Bonner turned back to Sterling. "Talkin' 'bout the Pinks?"

"Yep."

"Where are they?"

Sterling pointed to the south. "Oh…about three miles that way."

Bonner looked at Higgins and the others. "Well now, that makes it convenient."

Bubash nodded. "Gonna send the half-breed, Shadow Butler, and the Apache, Three Owls, 'long with you. The Injun knows the country…Ya'll shouldn't have much trouble takin' care of that bunch."

Big Slim looked at Bubash from under his bushy brows with his one good eye. "How many is there?"

"The two Pinkerton women, a deputy from Santa Fe, plus a man an' wife deputy sheriff team from Texas."

"Texas?"

"Yeah, they came out with the Pinkertons…Guess they're along for the ride."

Bonner exchanged glances again with his gang. "Three women an' two men? Haw! We'll give 'em a ride…Won't we boys?"

Higgins, Whitey, Zeke Burden, and Dime Box Mayfield grinned malevolently.

Sterling glared at the hired shootists. "Don't care what you do or how you do it, just want 'em off our tails...all of 'em."

Big Slim gave him his best imitation of a grin, considering the scar across his face as he bent down, picked up a cup sitting by the fire and filled it. "What we're here for."

An hour later, after resting and watering their horses, Three Owls, along with Shadow Butler, led Bonner's gang back out of the canyon and to the southwest.

"Me know good place for ambush Pinks, you follow."

Big Slim looked at the Apache and nodded. "Lead the way, Injun...right behind yuh."

They worked their way southeast over a saddle in the ridge surrounding the big caldera. Three Owls led them through the scattered cedar toward Cebollita Mesa and to an area of basalt outcrops interspersed with copses of juniper and piñon pines.

Big Slim looked around. "Damn, Injun, this *is* a good place for a ambush. That trail from the east leads right through here...Never see us till it's too late."

"Me know. This Apache country."

"Awright, listen up, you jackanapes scatter an' find some good hides on both sides of the trail. We'll have 'em in a crossfire." Bonner chuckled. "This ain't gonna take long."

Tyree led the group through the rugged area of scattered basalt thrusts, boulders, and cedar trees northwest along Redondo Creek in the direction of Cebollita Mesa.

Bone trotted Hildebrandt up beside Tyree. "Looks like prime country to get bushwhacked, doesn't it?"

"Is." Tyree nodded. "We go slow from here."

Silke motioned to the big black wolf-dog alongside her lineback dun. "Find 'em, Bear Dog, find 'em...go." She pointed ahead of them.

The almost psychic animal loped off ahead and disappeared around a grove of spruce.

Bone watched him fade into the brush and smiled. "Anybody up there, we'll dang sure know about it before they know we're here."

"He that good?"

"Ain't the half of it, Tyree. Like that Apache said back at the market in Santa Fe...Spirit wolf...Scares even me sometimes." Bone looked back at Silke. "Think he reads her mind."

The sun was settling toward the peaks to the west in front of them.

"Bad part is, sun's in our eyes."

"We can fix that, time comes, Tyree."

"Hope you're right, Bone. Back of my neck is itchin'."

"Yeah, mine too."

A half mile ahead of the Tyree led group, Big Slim and his gunmen had ensconced themselves on both sides of the trail. Some were behind boulders and others in thick copses of the low-growing piñons and cedars.

Bear Dog, belly low to the ground, glided through the thick brush. Suddenly he froze, thrust his nose up in the air for a moment, wheeled and headed back toward his mistress.

He stopped a hundred yards away on the other side of a large grove of mixed trees, trotted over to the middle of the trail, and waited until he heard their horses moving slowly closer. Bear Dog turned back to the west facing the direction of the ambushers, the hackles on his back rose.

Tyree held his hand up as they rounded a bend in the trail and spied Bear Dog in the trail ahead.

"Dang, he's better'n a bird dog on the point."

Bone grinned. "Told you he'd know, Tyree." He looked back at Silke, Haven, and Loraine. "Suggest we leave the horses here and go on foot."

Tyree nodded. "Agree with that, Bone."

They dismounted, loosened their girths a little and tied their mounts and Ted to some saplings off the trail.

Haven pulled her Cheyenne war bow from its sheath, strung it, and slipped the quiver of arrows over her head and left shoulder to hang at her back.

The others pulled their pistols from their holsters and loaded a final bullet in the cylinder, except Loraine who racked the slide on her Kimber 1911A semiautomatic.

Bone stood in the middle of the trail. "Alright, folks, listen up. We'll spread out through the trees on each side of the trail. Loraine and I will take the southwest side. Silke, you, Haven, and Tyree the northwest…You'll have Bear Dog with you…Since we don't know how many we're dealing with, let's try to keep quiet…both in movements and anything we have to do…unless you don't have a choice."

Haven raised her hand. "Like in takin' 'em out?"

He grinned sideways and raised an eyebrow. "What do you think?"

"Wish I had some of those knee-high Apache moccasins like the rest of ya'll do."

Bone glanced at him. "If the barkin' dog hadn't stopped to pee, Tyree, he'd caught the train."

"Do what?"

"Nothing…Let's move out. They'll be expecting us to be horseback in the trail…so they'll be where they can see it and we'll be behind them."

Silke grinned. "Surprise, surprise." She pulled the Chickasaw tomahawk from her belt and spun it around in her right hand.

He nodded. "That's the point." Bone glanced at Tyree. "See what I meant about fixing the sun in our eyes come time?"

"Yep."

Bone and Loraine moved to the opposite side of the trail.

"Pard, you head that way and let's stay at least twenty-five yards apart...watch your six."

"You watch yours," she replied as she disappeared around an outcrop of dark green schist.

Silke motioned Haven to her far right and Tyree to her left as she and Bear Dog vanished into thick junipers.

Haven pulled three steel-tipped arrows from her quiver, held two under her left hand on the grip of her bow and notched the third in the sinew string.

She crept toe-heel through the needle carpeted brush closer to where they thought the ambushers would be, eyes alert for anything that didn't belong—Haven froze...

Up the trail several hundred yards, Loraine turned sideways to go between two large cedars and literally bumped into the back of one of the drygulchers, the half-breed, Shadow Butler, on the other side.

"Son-of-a…" Butler exclaimed as he wheeled around, his rifle pointed at her stomach.

Loraine's training as a seventh degree black belt Kung Fu artist automatically activated as she swung a roundhouse kick to the center of the Winchester, knocking it spinning out of his hands.

He quickly drew his ten inch Bowie and went into a knife fighting stance with an evil, confident grin. "Ohh, bitch, gonna gut you like a deer."

"Not likely, scum-bag."

Loraine, dropped her rifle, executed a 360 degree spin kick with her left leg to his head, staggering him to the side. While he was off-balance, she used the heel of her right hand and drove it under his nose, snapping his head back and crushing the cartilage.

She whipped her left arm around his knife hand, grabbed his wrist, spun him about and used his momentum to drive his own knife into his stomach—she twisted his wrist and pulled up, slicing through a lung and into his heart with the top of the razor-edged clip blade.

Shadow's eyes went wide as he tried to suck in a breath that wasn't there and collapsed at her feet like so much dirty laundry—dead.

Loraine looked down at him. "Told you."

§§§

CHAPTER TWENTY

VALLES CALDERA

Marvin Bubash an' Rudolph Sterling sat in camp chairs in front of their tent, sipping on gill glasses of brandy.

Sterling picked up the bottle from the small table between their chairs, refilled his glass and looked at his partner. "Need a freshen?"

Bubash nodded and held out his glass. "Should be hearing gunfire just anytime now."

"Well, I was thinking we already should have." Sterling pulled out his gold pocket watch, popped the cover and looked at the face. "'Bout fifteen minutes ago."

"Maybe those Pinks weren't making as much time as we thought."

Sterling took a sip. "Could be."

Haven stared down at a four foot long Western Diamondback Rattlesnake just a single step in front of her in the narrow path through the junipers. He was thicker of body than her arm and coiled to strike any intruder who dared to interrupt his sunning.

His tail, with ten rattles and a button, shook an ominous warning to her as his forked tongue flicked in and out of his wide, evil-looking triangle-shaped head.

She slowly backed away out of his strike zone which was almost the full length of his body. "You want the trail, big boy, you got it. No argument from me...I'll go another way."

Haven carefully stepped around the big cedar in case he had a friend or two close by, and stealthily moved toward the area Bear Dog had been focused on.

Tyree slipped around a low hogback of mostly obsidian that was just above head high. He quietly approached Zeke Burden who was standing behind another upthrust with his Henry braced on top, pointing at the trail below.

A small rock rolled under Tyree's booted foot alerting the short outlaw there was someone behind him. He spun around.

Tyree rushed him with his knife drawn as Burden pulled his Colt.

Burden grabbed Tyree's wrist above his knife hand while the deputy held the drygulcher's gun arm.

They wrestled about like in some odd dance until Tyree drove his forehead into Burden's face, crushing his nose. Blood squirted from the man's nostrils as he released his grip and staggered back.

He shook his head and raised his gun to point it at Tyree's stomach only four feet away—and thumbed the hammer back…

Haven squatted down in the shadow of a juniper and studied the boulders and thrusts close to the trail for a moment, looking for any movement—and was shortly rewarded.

The top of a man's head, sans his hat, briefly appeared from between two large, dark, basalt boulders, and then disappeared back down—his hair was snow white. He did it again, focusing on the trail below him each time.

Dang, that's not long enough…Oh, I know. She started whistling the melody to a popular song, 'Listen to the Mockingbird'.

The white-haired head popped up and scanned the area.

Haven stood, drew the Cheyenne war bow to the long hunting arrow's full length. She touched the fletched end of the deadly missile and the three fingertips of her right hand to her cheek briefly—then released it.

The steel-tipped arrow designed for killing buffalo, other big game—or men—flew true. It struck Whitey Loretto just in front of and above his left ear and passed almost its full length through his skull.

He dropped like a pile of wet newspaper where he stood—only his left heel moved after he hit the ground as it drummed a short tattoo in the sandy soil.

"One down." Haven took another arrow from her left hand, notched it on the string and quickly looked around.

She jumped at the sound of a pistol shot. "Uh-oh."

Tyree had thrown his ten inch Bowie at Zeke Burden's chest, impaling it almost to the hilt after making one rotation.

Zeke squeezed the trigger on his Army Colt as he collapsed—dead when he hit the ground. The bullet kicked up a spume of sand as it impacted two feet in front of him.

Bubash looked at Sterling. "Wasn't that a gunshot?"

Rudolph grinned and nodded. "It was...but a pistol shot. Was expecting rifle fire."

"And only one?"

Sterling frowned and looked off to the south. "Yeah...only one."

Silke turned in the direction of the gunfire. "Oh, damn." *Now they're gonna be on the alert.*

She waved Bear Dog off up the trail and peered through the branches of a piñon pine at Dime Box Mayfield looking all around his location, his Winchester in his hands at his hip. There was a questioning look on his face.

He glanced back around the ponderosa pine he was in back of above the trail, and then behind him into the forest, but couldn't see Silke in the shadows. Her tan buckskins blended into the trunks of the other trees.

Gotta make this quick. She stepped out from behind the tree. "Hey!"

Dime Box, standing well over forty feet away, whipped around with his rifle at his hip.

Silke executed an overhand toss of her war hatchet, it flipped three times before burying its razor sharp blade in the center of Mayfield's forehead, snapping it back and causing his body to slam against the trunk of the tree. He slumped to the ground without a sound.

She glanced around and stepped forward to his body. Silke placed her moccasined foot in the middle of his chest, grabbed the wooden handle of the tomahawk and wrenched it from the bone with a slight popping sound.

Hank Higgins crept through some boulders from fifty yards away coming in the direction of Dime Box after hearing Silke's, 'Hey!'. His rifle was at the ready. He spied her standing over his friend's body and brought the Winchester to his shoulder...

"Ah, that's what I've been waiting to hear, rifle fire." Sterling took another sip of his brandy.

Bubash cocked his head and listened intently. "But again, only one...That's two altogether. This ain't right, Sterling."

Rudolph ground his teeth and glared at Bubash.

One hundred pounds of black fury impacted Higgins as he pulled the trigger, causing the shot to go high.

Higgins went down with Bear Dog on top of him, rending and tearing with his inch and half long fangs. He was screaming like a terrified woman as he futilely tried to fend the wolf-dog away from his face and throat—he lost.

Bear Dog's huge jaws clamped on Higgins lower face and throat and closed with a crunching sound as bone and cartilage collapsed. Blood sprayed from his severed jugular while his entire throat was torn out. He died in a large pool of his own blood.

Three Owls heard the two shots, and then the screams of one of the other men. He left his post and headed back toward the area where they had tethered their horses.

Big Slim Bonner, with no slight modicum of consternation showing in his face knowing the ambush was a failure, also headed toward the horses.

"Where you going, bub?"

The barrel-chested man turned to face Bone as he stepped out from around a boulder only five feet away.

"Who the hell are you?"

Bone grinned. "Deputy Bone…and I'm your worst nightmare."

"Hell you say." Bonner charged Bone with his head down, thinking to bull rush him.

Bone stepped to the side and pushed his head down as he went by. Bonner did a face plant in the dirt.

He got to his feet, turned to face Bone and spat dirt and grass from his mouth. "What's the matter, big man, afraid to fight?"

"Oh, I'll fight you all right, but you're not goin' to like it."

"Let's see what you got, then, lawdog." He took a roundhouse swing at Bone's head.

Bone blocked it with his left arm and jabbed Big Slim in the middle of his face with his right, smashing his nose, splattering blood in all directions.

"Damn you."

Bonner swung again, this time a little quicker than Bone expected and caught him a glancing blow on his cheek, staggering him.

Bone stepped back and shook his head to clear the stars. "Good shot."

Bonner spat blood from his mouth. "That's just a start." He swung again and bounced his ham-like fist from Bone's forehead.

He was staggered again and went into a defensive circling strategy, jabbing Big Slim in the face with his left quicker than the man could block them.

Bone stepped in when Bonner raised both hands to protect his face and drove a powerful right to his ribs.

Big Slim bent to the side and groaned, then Bone countered with a left to his ear, spinning him around. He came back with another right to Bonner's solar plexus driving the air from his lungs and staggering him back where he dropped to his knees.

He sucked in air to his starving lungs, looked up at Bone with his one eye and snarled. "I'm done with this."

Bonner jerked his Remington .44 from his holster, thumbing the hammer back as he brought it to shoulder level.

Bone was caught off guard, but still tried to unsnap the safety strap over the hammer of his Smith and Wesson 500.

Before he could draw, six inches of a feathered shaft was protruding from the middle of Bonner's chest with another twenty inches of a steel-shod arrow sticking out of his back.

A surprise look came over Big Slim's face as he looked down at the arrow, and then back up at Haven behind Bone when she stepped out of the trees.

"One of them damned Pink…"

He never finished as he fell forward, dead.

Bone and Haven heard hoof beats thundering down the trail below them. They both rushed over to see Three Owls kicking his overo paint horse in the ribs as they galloped away almost seventy yards distance.

Haven notched another arrow, drew it back to full draw, raised her aim above and ahead of the galloping Apache and released her fingers.

They watched as the arrow arched up, and then down to the Indian trying to escape and buried half its length in his low back.

Three Owls lurched forward but somehow managed to stay in the saddle as he and the horse disappeared around a bend.

Bone looked over at Haven in wonder and admiration. "Dang girl, that was almost a hundred yard shot…You're kinda handy with that thing."

She blushed as Silke, Tyree, Loraine, and Bear Dog stepped out from the trees behind them.

Silke had a big grin on her face. "Been practicin', huh, cuz?"

A red-faced Haven Justice grinned. "A little."

§§§

CHAPTER TWENTY-ONE

VALLES CALDERA

Bubash and Sterling jumped to their feet as Three Owls' lathered horse trotted into the camp and stopped. Her sides heaved as the exhausted animal tried to catch his wind.

The Apache was slumped over in the saddle, head on the right side of the horse's neck, his hands intertwined in the mane. The reins were draped loosely around the horse's neck.

Ollie Wilkes and Tater Adams joined the two men as they ran up to the quivering horse.

"What the hell?...He's got an arrow in his back," Ollie reached up to pull Three Owls from the saddle.

Tater put his hand on Ollie's arm. "Hold it...Good God amighty...arrow's got him pinned to the saddle. Went plumb through him an' into the swell."

"Well, break it off, fool," said Sterling.

Ollie reached in between the Indian's body and the saddle with his Bowie and cut the shaft where it was imbedded in the swell below the pommel.

Tater and Bubash eased him from the saddle to the ground on his left side. The end of the arrow still protruded from his back.

Sterling pointed. "Should be able to pull that shaft out now that the head's gone." He glanced around. "Bring some rags. Gonna bleed some."

Coon Creede and Jess Shepherd brought a shirt and some clean longjohns from their saddlebags and handed them to Ollie.

Wilkes wrapped his hand around the feathers. "Hold 'im."

He ripped the white cotton tunic away from the wound, gave the shaft a hard jerk and pulled it through the Indian's body. Three Owls jumped and let out a moan. His eyes fluttered several times while Ollie pressed a folded torn leg from the longjohns against the back hole and the other leg on the front exit wound to try and stop the bleeding. The blood was almost black, indicating the arrow went through the liver.

Tater held a canteen to the man's lips and let him have a few sips.

Sterling leaned into the Apache's face and shook his shoulder. "Three Owls...what the hell happened?"

He groaned as he swallowed. "Kill all."

"Ya'll killed them all?"

Three Owls slowly shook his head. "No, she-devils an' deputies kill all...even Three Owls." He sucked a breath of air in, and then slowly exhaled in a death rattle as life left his body. "Ahhhh."

Wilkes looked at the bloody arrow still in his hand. "Huh…interstin'. This here's a 'Pache arrow."

Loraine wet her kerchief with some water from one of their canteens. Haven and Tyree had brought their horses up. She cleaned the dirt from Bone's face and the blood from a small gash on his cheek.

Bone winced. "Ow, Babe, not so hard."

"You should have ducked…Now, be still. You need to start doing some of that Kung Fu that I've taught you."

"Yes, Ma'am…was trying, but he didn't want to cooperate." He glanced at the others. "I just want to know how the hell they knew that we were coming…an' where we were."

Silke nodded. "Good question."

Tyree scratched the stubble on his chin. "Well, mebe, this is the way to their camp…an' mebe they had these fellers staked out here in case anybody was comin' their way…an' mebe they just figured we wuz comin'…an' mebe they don't know 'bout the gals escapin'."

Haven grunted. "An' mebe there *is* an Easter Bunny."

Silke bent over and studied Big Slim's bruised face. "Well, well."

"What?"

She looked at Bone, and then at Haven. "I know who this is."

"Are you going to keep us in the dark or is this a guessin' game?...Ow!" He looked at Loraine again.

"This is Big Slim Bonner."

Haven frowned. "Big Slim Bonner?"

Silke nodded. "Yep, Bull Bonner's younger brother..."

"The Bonner-Crossfield gang?"

"Correct, Loraine."

"Saw some fliers on them before we left Gainesville...Thought ya'll and Marshal Selden Lindsey took care of that bunch up in Colorado last week?"

"Did...Bull's brother, Big Slim here, wasn't with 'em."

"Big Slim don't really go together, does it?"

"Is kind of a paradox, I'd say."

Tyree looked at Bone. "A what?"

"A paradox...wrapped in an enigma, surrounded by a riddle..."

"Be right proud you'd speak English, Bone."

"An oxymoron..." He looked at Tyree's confusion. "A contradiction of terms."

"Oh, you mean they're opposite...Been a lot easier to just say so." Tyree looked down at the dead outlaw. "Then mebe he follered you gals down here after ya'll help kill his brother an' his gang?"

Bone grimaced. "That's still thin as a soup sandwich."

Silke glanced around at the others. "May never know."

Haven shrugged. "Then again...we might...Gonna do anything 'bout the bodies?"

Bone shook his head. "Those girls are more important. We can tell the sheriff about 'em later, he can send out the undertaker with a wagon...for whatever's left." He looked up at the turkey buzzards already circling overhead.

"Reckon there's any bounty?"

"Is on this Big Slim Bonner character, Haven...a thousand dollars. Saw a dodger on 'im couple weeks ago...Need to look an' see who the others are 'fore we go…Bettin' some of them got bounties, too."

"Think the word of three sheriff's deputies should suffice for identification…" Bone looked at Loraine. "Don't you, Babe?"

"I would imagine."

"Need to see as I can salvage my arrow…only got twenty to start with…an' used three, countin' this one…"

"Let me see if'n I kin pull it through, Haven."

"Would appreciate that, Tyree."

He stepped over and rolled Big Slim's body to the side, held the man's shoulder, and pulled from the backside since the head was completely through. The feathered end disappeared into his chest as Tyree pulled it out the back. He held the bloody shaft up.

"Think we better see as we kin wash some of the blood off…Feathers still attached. Well made, I'd say."

Haven smiled. "'Preciate it, Tyree." She unscrewed the cap on her canteen and poured water along the shaft, especially over the feathers.

Tyree rubbed as much of the blood off with his fingers as he could.

She pecked him on the cheek. "Thank you, Tyree."

He blushed and ducked his head. "Yessum."

"Just have to let it dry a bit before I put it back in my quiver.

They worked their way to each of the bodies. The first, since it was the closest, was the ambusher Loraine killed.

Tyree knelt down and rolled the body over. "Shadow Butler, half-breed, ne'er-do-well around Santa Fe...No bounty I know 'bout."

Silke looked at the others. "Who's next?"

"Probably mine." Tyree pointed. "I was yonder some but no need in goin' over there, already know who it was...Zeke Burden. He's got two hundert on his head...dead or alive."

Silke nodded. "Awright, then where?"

"Me." Haven strode off up the trail. "This way. Nailed a white-headed guy."

Tyree grinned. "Dollar to a bear sign, it's Whitey Loretto."

They pushed through the cedar trees to the body lying between two boulders.

Tyree looked down at the body. "Dadgum, girl...Right through the head. Ol' Whitey never knew what hit 'im...Got five hundert on his head. Been lookin' for 'im...Murder, stagecoach robbery, rape."

"Nice fella." Bone glanced at Haven. "Good shootin' girl...How'd you get the shot?"

She grinned. "Whistled a tune an' when he stood up to look around..."

"Huh, sounds like Sergeant York."

"Who, Bone?"

"Uh...Oh, guy I heard about, Tyree. Made a sound like a gobbling turkey to shoot some, uh...bad guys."

"Hmm, good trick. Have to 'member that."

"Right." Bone and Loraine exchanged glances and grins.

Silke pointed. "I was over here." She led the way, twisting around and through scattered boulders and piñon pine to the body.

"Whoa! Would you look at that? Tomahawk dead center 'tween his eyes...Good throw, Silke. Where'd you learn that?"

"I was inducted into the Hatchet Woman Warrior Clan of the Chickasaw last year. My mentor, Lighthorse Red Wolf, taught me."

"Chickasaw has woman warrior clans?"

"Uh-huh, two. The Hatchet Woman Clan and the Panther Woman Clan...They're considered equal to the men warriors."

"Wow, who knew?...Anyway, this here's Dime Box Mayfield from up Kansas way."

"What all's he done?" asked Silke.

"Cheap grifter, petty theft, stagecoach robbery...Only got a hundert on him."

Bone shrugged. "Beats a poke in the eye with a sharp stick."

Tyree looked at him. "Do what?"

"Nothin'."

"That everybody?" asked Tyree.

"Heard Bear Dog get somebody just to the north of here...Don't think it's far." Silke took off through the bushes.

Bear Dog seemed to know where she was headed as he ran in front of her the fifty yards to his kill. He stood beside the body, dancing on his front feet, wagging his tail as if to say, 'Here's mine, here's mine'.

Tyree looked at the gory scene, Haven turned around and gagged.

"Oh, my." He looked at the smiling Bear Dog. "Think he enjoys his work." He bent over and studied what was left of the man's face. "Well, well...Near as I can tell, what with the bottom of his face gone an' all...this'd be Hank Higgins. Bonner's right hand man an' just about as bad...Murder, cattle an' horse rustlin', bank robbery, arson, you name it...Worth a thousand, too, like Bonner."

Loraine held up a small wire-bound notebook. "Got all of them written down...Comes to twenty-eight hundred dollars."

"Think there's goin' to be some more...Now let's go find those girls. Come on Bear Dog." Silke headed back toward the horses.

§§§

CHAPTER TWENTY-TWO

VALLES CALDERA

Sterling looked up from Three Owls' body. "I think we should load the merchandise in the wagon and leave this place."

Bubash returned his look. "Reckon they're comin'?"

"What the hell do you think?"

"You believe they can find us?"

Sterling nodded. "Damn sure do. They're coming this way and that deputy of Sheriff Russell knows this area…Think it's just a matter of time."

"Where do we go?"

"To the rendezvous point. Be a day early but that should be all right."

Bubash glanced down at the Apache's body. "Beats not at all…Coon, get Jess and ya'll hook the wagon up. Tater, you an Moose bring the girls down…He's still up there guardin' 'em."

"What 'bout Murphy watchin' the entrance?"

Bubash shook his head. "Coon, don't you think he'll know to join up with us on the way out?"

"Oh, yeah, reckon that's right."

"Glad you concur…Now get on about it."

"Yessir…Uh, what 'bout Three Owls' body an' his horse there?"

"Leave 'em. Don't have time to bury him an' that horse's too spent to be any good right now. Strip the tack an' let her go…She'll either get better an' join a wild herd somewheres or she won't."

Coon looked at the well-built yellow and white overo mare and grimaced as he pulled the bridle from her head, and then unwrapped the latigo from the horsehair cinch O ring. "Damn nice mare." He set the saddle on the ground, slid the sweat-soaked blanket off, and draped it over the saddle—wet side up. "Go girl." He slapped her butt and she headed direct to the creek for some much needed water.

Silke trotted *Lakná* up beside Bone's Hildebrandt. "Think the girls are still where Sheriff Russell left 'em?"

Bone shrugged. "Don't know but we have to check where he said and go from there."

"Suppose so but got a bad feelin'."

He pinched his lips. "Me too."

Silke nodded and glanced down at Bear Dog padding alongside them. "Find, Bear Dog, find." She waved him forward.

"Good idea in case there's any more of those miscreants out there in front of us."

"My thoughts, too."

Tyree led the bunch along the game trail that tracked northwest mostly through the sometimes dense woods and sometimes up a little past the tree line and the shinnery.

"How far you think we're from the girl's hidin' place, Tyree?"

He grinned, showing his even white teeth and smoothed his mustache with his index finger. "Well, Haven, if'n I were a bettin' man...which I ain't, by the way...but if'n I wuz, I'd say 'bout another two mile." Tyree turned in his saddle to the others behind him. "Mind we oughta give the stock a blow up yonder at that meadow next to the stream."

Bone nodded. "Agreed. Trackin' sideways across the face of this ridge is pretty rough on 'em, even Ted."

They pulled rein close to the edge of the babbling stream as it flowed down the hillside tumbling over rounded rocks and boulders.

Tyree stepped down from Laddie. "Let's strip the gear an' give everbody a good rubdown with some of that long grass, then let 'em graze a spell."

"I'll fix a pot of coffee if somebody'll gather some firewood," said Loraine.

Bone grinned as he dismounted and started pulling the tack from his seventeen hand gelding. "Thought you'd never bring it up, Babe."

"I'll give the big boy a good rubdown after I do *d'Artagnan*, Bone, if you want to go ahead an' gather Loraine's wood."

"Deal, Haven…Sure ready for a cup of her java."

"Wonder how come they call coffee, *java*? Heard that most of my life."

"Well, back in the 1600s they found it grew exceptionally well in Java. That's a large island in the Dutch East Indies archipelago of Malaysia…It soon became one of the leadin' suppliers in the world of the tasty little beans we roast and grind down to make coffee."

"How do you know all that kind of stuff?"

"It's a gift."

She smiled. "Not gonna be a quiz, is there?"

Bone shrugged. "Haven't decided yet…Let you know."

"You do that," she said as she led Hildebrandt over to the others.

Everyone either sat crosslegged on the ground or knelt on one knee, drinking their hot coffee. Bear Dog lay beside Silke, his head on his paws out in front of him.

Tyree pitched the remains of his coffee, mostly grounds, in the fire. "Should be there by sundown, my figurin's right…Let's saddle up."

Haven got to her feet and did the same with her dregs. "Sure hope the girls are awright."

"Find out shortly," commented Loraine.

Bear Dog shot to his feet, the hair on his back instantly shot erect. A low growl rumbled from deep in his throat. He stared across the stream into the thick, dark woods.

Haven pointed. "Look! What's that?"

"What?" Silke stood and looked where she was pointing.

Haven glanced at her, then Tyree. "You see it?"

He raised his eyebrows. "Saw somethin' but not long enough to figure out what it was. Movin' on four feet…Too big for a wolf an' too fast for a bear."

"Mountain lion?"

Haven shook her head. "Too big for that too, Bone."

Bear Dog whined and looked up at Silke.

She knelt down and caressed his head and back. "He's shakin'…Like he did back in that cave the other night."

"Could you tell what color it was?" asked Loraine.

Tyree shook his head. "Coulda been black but it was in the shadows…Be any color, black, brown…gray…"

Silke looked up from Bear Dog. "Whatever it was is gone, he's not shakin' anymore."

Tyree pursed his lips and muttered, "Skinwalker."

"Wish you hadn't said that."

"Well, is what it is, Haven…the Navajo think they can shapeshift into anythin' they want to be."

Bone walked over to the gear and picked up his saddle and blanket. "Two of ya'll saw something and don't think Bear Dog is subject to seeing things that aren't there…Look yonder at the horses and Ted."

All of the animals were facing the woods and stomping their front feet or snorting nervously.

"Glad we hobbled 'em…" Tyree picked up his saddle and blanket, too. "…or we might be spendin' the rest of the afternoon lookin' for 'em."

"Good point," added Loraine.

Tater and Moose led the eleven girls to the back of the freight wagon hooked to a team of black nose Tennessee mules. The sideboards were three feet high.

Moose lowered the tailgate and helped the girls up one at time. "Ya'll sit down there 'long the sides an' be still er I'll be a tyin' yuh up."

Yellow Bird and Sarah were the last two to get in. Moose clambered in after them as Tater handed him his rifle, lifted the tailgate up and latched it.

He tied his and Moose's horses to the iron rings on the back, then he walked to the right side of the front and stepped up to the driver's bench.

Bubash and Sterling led the way out with Ollie Wilkes, Coon Creede, and Jess Shepherd following behind the wagon.

Al Murphy climbed down from the ledge where he had been stationed, mounted his horse that had been tethered below and fell in beside Shepherd.

"Leavin' early, huh?"

Coon nodded to Murphy. "Three Owls tol' us them Pinks an' deputies wiped out Big Slim Bonner an' the bunch of 'em 'fore he died. Figured we needed to go on to the rendezvous place."

"You don't say?"

"Do."

"Them Pinks an'em must be some kinda curly wolves...Seen Three Owls come in all slumped over in his saddle."

"An' they're women on top of it all."

Murphy twisted around to look over at Shepherd, his eyes widened. "Naw! Get out from here...Yer funnin' me...Women?"

Jess nodded. "What Big Slim said...The two Pinkertons is young, cain't be mor'n twenty-two er three an' one of the deputies is a little Mescan gal not much bigger'n a nickle."

"An' they took out Big Slim's gang 'long with the breed an' the 'Pache?"

Coon Creede nodded. "That's a fact er God's a possum."

Murphy shook his head. "Damnation...Gals sound like that lady law I heered 'bout from up in the Nations...Deputy Marshal Fiona Miller. Hear tell she'd tangle with ol' Scratch his ownself…Don't backwater to no man."

"Women takin' over everthin'. I even heered they give 'em the right to vote up in Wyomin'," said Shepherd.

Coon spat a long stream of amber tobacco juice off the side of the trail at a rock. "Had my druthers, druther tangle with Bass Reeves er Wyatt Earp, er even a mad bobcat than a woman on the prod."

"Damn shore got that right. Marshal Reeves won't shoot yuh less'n yer shootin' at him. Woman…why they ain't no reas'nin' with a pissed off woman. Jest as well check yer soul to God, 'cause yer butt's hers."

"Amen to that, Shepherd, amen to that," agreed Murphy. "What's the world comin' to?"

Tater turned the team to the northwest following Bubash and Sterling in a loop around to San Antonio Mountain over four miles away.

A brief wry grin flashed across Sarah's face as she listened to the men behind the wagon.

§§§

CHAPTER TWENTY-THREE

VALLES CALDERA

Bone dropped Hildebrandt's reins, ground-tying him. "Gonna check something out…Haven, why don't you come show me where you saw that thing?"

"Sure, Bone."

They walked to the eight foot wide gurgling stream and Bone picked out some rocks to step on to get across without getting their feet wet. Haven followed behind.

"This way." She led him over to an area a good twenty-five feet from the stream into the trees.

Bone scanned the soft earth around where Haven indicated. "Hah!…Good golly Miss Molly. Look at this." He knelt down and pointed.

She leaned over to look at the track. "What in the world is it?"

He shook his head. "That's…a Wolf track."

Haven straightened up and looked at him. "That big?"

Bone nodded. "Yeah…Come on. Seen all I need to see." He stepped to the stream, then crossed back over.

Silke looked up from tightening her cinch. "Find somethin'?"

"Could say."

Loraine shook her head. "He always does this."

"What?" asked Tyree.

"Wants us to prise it out of him…Damn you, Bone, just tell us."

"Found wolf tracks."

Tyree shook his head. "No way…that creature was way too big."

Bone held up his hands and made a big circle with his forefingers and thumbs the size of a saucer. "Yep, about twice the size of Bear Dog's paws. Had to be between two and three hundred pounds."

"Oh, get out."

"Count on it, Silke. They're known as Dire Wolves…The catch is they've been extinct for around 10,000 years. Not long after the first Amerindians showed up…the Clovis and Folsom cultures…the predecessors to the Anasazi."

She shook her head. "But how…"

Tyree interrupted her. "Like I said earlier…Shapeshifters…They can take on any form, as the Navajo say. One of their favorites is a giant wolf…"

Loraine pinched her lips. "The Europeans call them Lycanthrope…Werewolves."

"Ooo!" Haven looked back across the brook. "So you're sayin' Shapeshifters are worldwide?"

Bone nodded. "Every civilization since the ancient Samaritans has legends of them…including the aborigines in Australia."

"All myths and legends have a basis of fact somewhere," said Silke.

Bone smiled. "More or less…Well, shall we go, people?" He stuck his foot in the stirrup and swung up into the big gelding's saddle. "Regardless, we need to find those girls."

Tyree led the way out of the small clearing to the northwest.

SAN ANTONIO MOUNTAIN

Tater followed Bubash and Sterling up to the mountain rendezvous and pulled the team to a halt next to a large light gray rhyolite ridge near the base. There was another outcrop almost a hundred yards away forming a semi-protective cul-de-sac of volcanic rock with a small stream running almost in the center.

Sterling stepped down from his mount and turned to the rest of the gunhands. "All right, spread out. Find some good positions of cover on those ridges an' keep your eyes peeled."

Tater unhooked the team and picketed them near the water on some graze.

Moose clambered over the tail gate to the ground, turned around, unhooked it, and let it down. "Awright ladies, out. Sit down over yonder next to the face of that outcrop...an' keep quiet."

The girls, some holding hands, walked over to the rock face, sat down, looking around fearfully.

Bubash glanced up at the sun as it was settling toward the horizon on the other side of San Antonio Mountain, sending long fingers of shadows across the caldera, and showing red and silver linings on the scattered clouds.

He started making a fire ring of stones. "I'll get a fire started for some coffee and supper...Moose, you want to rustle up some deadfall an' blowdown?"

"Shorething, Boss." He sauntered off into the brush and scattered trees.

VALLES CALDERA

"Sure this is the place, Tyree?" Silke looked around the small clearing next to the babbling stream.

Tyree got down and studied the ground along the trail. "No question, see a bunch of small footprints..." He looked up and pinched his lips. "Saw the sheriff's tracks but there's also tracks of five or six men on top. I'd say, the kidnappers found 'em...yesterd'y late."

Silke hung her head in exasperation and blew her cheeks out. "Oh, me." She looked up and back at Tyree. "Which way did they go?"

"Back up the ridge to the crest an' over to the other side. They wuz all afoot...we'll have to go around."

Bone stepped down. "Any guess as to where they went?"

Tyree nodded. "Mind they went to some abandoned cliff dwellin's on the other side of this ridge. There's several...Have to check 'em all."

Silke looked over at the setting sun. "Be dark soon...It'll get dark real quick once the sun gets behind the mountains."

Bone nodded. "Just as well make camp here. No moon tonight till around three or four, and then only a horned moon...be black as pitch."

"Darned if we do and darned if we don't," added Loraine as she also dismounted.

Tyree started pulling his tack. "Well, got water an' graze...Start ag'in at daybreak."

"When do ya'll think the sheriff will be back?" asked Haven.

"'Pends on how far he had to go to find a wagon big enough. However far...be the same back," answered Tyree. "May have had to go all the way to Sante Fe...forty mile er so."

Bone pulled his saddle and blanket and laid them over near the trees. "Late tomorrow at best." He took a piece of burlap from his saddlebags and gave Hildebrandt a good rubdown.

The others followed suit and hobbled their mounts and Ted on the fresh grass. The late afternoon sounds of frogs from the stream, night birds, cicadas, and crickets began to dominate the early evening. Squirrels were fussing and chattering in the trees, finishing up the day's hunt for food.

Loraine had the fire going, the coffee on, and was building a stew from chopped jerky, wild onions, piñon nuts, mushrooms, and cattail roots—with a few pinches of salt and ground pepper.

Bone walked up with another armload of deadfall and dropped it next to the fire pit. "Coffee ready, Babe?"

"It is…Help yourself." She stirred the stew with a wooden spoon.

Bone leaned over and smelled. "Yum…amazing what you can do with a few fixin's."

She flashed her large brown eyes at the big man. "Some of us have talent…and some don't."

"Ouch." He grinned, imitated the sound of an arrow striking his chest with his fist, turned and kissed her on the side of her neck.

Loraine's body quivered. "Ooh, damn you, Bone, you know what that does to me."

He flicked his eyebrows several times. "Yeah."

She winked at him. "Later."

"Works for me." He took a sip of his coffee.

It was well past gloaming when across the bubbling stream, a pack of coyotes began tuning up for their nightly hunt.

Haven walked over to the fire and poured herself another cup of after-dinner coffee and looked up at the serenade. "Wonder why they do that?"

Tyree glanced over at her. "What's that?"

"All that yippin', yappin', an' hollerin'."

"You don't know?"

She frowned and looked at him from under her dark eyebrows.

He smiled. "Well, Haven, they get together each night and divi up by drawin' straws to see who hunts where…an' all that hollerin' is 'cause they don't have no thumbs fer the draw." He stirred the fire in front of him with a stick, sending a shower of sparks swirling into the air.

Haven picked up a small rock and chunked at him, bouncing it off his shoulder.

"Ow."

Silke sprayed her coffee out in front of her while Bone snorted his out of his nose.

Loraine giggled, and then looked at the darkening woods around them as they abruptly went stone cold quiet. "What the…"

Bear Dog shot to his feet beside the fire, eyes focused across the stream, and a growl emanated from deep in his throat.

Haven pointed. "Look, there it is again."

This time they all caught a quick glimpse of a large four-legged creature slinking through the shadows before it disappeared.

"Dangnation, that's definitely a wolf...A giant one like Bone said," commented Tyree.

"Sure shut the coyotes water off," added Bone.

Silke nodded. "And everything else."

SAN ANTONIO MOUNTAIN

Bubash stirred the beans and bacon in the skillet on a flat rock close to the flames. The night sounds proliferated and filled the darkness as elsewhere in the wide caldera.

Another group of coyotes, like across the caldera at Silke's camp, were exchanging howls and yips.

"Sounds like a big pack, probably ten or fifteen," noted Sterling. "Glad they do that early...no sleeping when they're singing."

Suddenly, they stopped. The silence quickly became palpable as the frogs and other night creatures also went silent.

ANGEL JUSTICE

A high piercing scream, followed by another, rent the quiet as Yellow Bird and Sally Ann grabbed each other.

Sarah pointed at two glowing red eyes almost four feet off the ground staring at them from the other side of the camp...

§§§

CHAPTER TWENTY-FOUR

VALLES CALDERA

Thirty minutes after the sighting of the creature, the sounds of the night slowly returned. First the frogs, then the rhythmic buzzing of the cicadas, the crickets, and night birds—even the coyotes started their mournful serenade again.

Tyree took a sip of his cold coffee, made a face, spat it out on the ground, and refilled his cup from the pot. "Reckon the Navajo have a point 'bout their stories on Skinwalkers."

"Think it was the same one as we saw earlier?"

Tyree looked at Haven. "No way of tellin'...Don't even know if it's real flesh an' blood or..."

Silke turned from staring at the woods. "Or what?...Some phantasm or wraith...Or did we all just imagine we saw somethin'."

Bone cleared his throat. "Don't think Bear Dog and all the other creatures in the woods would be subject to our imaginations...collective or not."

"And you said the Dire Wolf has been extinct for 10,000 years?" asked Loraine.

"To quote Shakespeare in *Hamlet*, 'There are more things in heaven and Earth, Horatio, than are dreamt of in your philosophy.'."

"You gotta quit calling me Horatio, Silke."

She grinned. "Beats some other things I could think of, Bone."

"That's right, pick on the big guy."

"Well, whatever it is, it doesn't seem to be aggressive or threatenin' towards us," commented Haven.

"Yet."

They all looked at Loraine as she raised her dark eyebrows.

SAN ANTONIO MOUNTAIN

The two glowing red eyes disappeared as quickly as they appeared.

Bubash looked at Sterling. "What the sam hill was that?"

"DamnifIknow."

"*Yee naaldooshii.*"

The men looked over at Yellow Bird as she leaned back from her embrace with Sally Ann.

"What's that, Injun?" asked Sterling.

"Skinwalker."

"Means 'he who walk on all fours'...evil spirit...witches," said another Navajo, Moon Water.

"Balderdash." Sterling got to his feet and looked into the darkness where the eyes had been.

"Probably a young bear with the fire catching his eyes."

Yellow Bird and Moon Water exchanged knowing glances.

VALLES CALDERA

The eastern sky turned a flat gray with a pink lining growing at the horizon and red and gold arrows shooting up signaling the coming sun.

Loraine stirred the night coals of the fire into flames by adding twigs, then sticks before laying a couple of larger pieces of deadfall on top. They immediately began to crackle and pop.

She carried the blue speckled graniteware pot over to the clear stream, filled it, walked back to the fire, and set it on a flat rock close to the flames.

Tyree stepped out of the woods where he had gone to take care of his morning business and picked up an armfull of dry branches. "Need some more wood, Loraine?"

"I will, Tyree, thanks." She glanced over at Bone still snoozing in his blankets and smiled. "He's not really a morning person."

"I can tell...Looks like the events of last night didn't bother him none."

"Nothing does when it comes to him sleepin'. Think he could sleep standing up."

"He was in combat in the Marines, wasn't he?"

"He was."

Tyree nodded. "You learn to sleep anywhere, anytime in combat, because you sleep with one eye open...Tend to live longer thataway."

"That's what he says."

"Ya'll think I don't hear you, but I got every word."

Tyree and Loraine looked back over at Bone—his eyes were still closed.

Bear Dog glanced first at Bone, then at Tyree, and finally at Loraine.

Tyree laughed. "Think Bear Dog's tryin' to figure out what's goin' on."

Bone threw his blanket back and sat up. "Just as well get up, then, since ya'll won't give a man any peace."

"What's the matter, hon, not sleep as well as normal?"

"No, slept fine...Just that I got up twice during the night. Bear Dog and I made a circle around the camp and the horses couple times while ya'll were cuttin' 'Zs'."

Tyree shook his head. "Huh…I usually know when anyone is movin' 'round at night."

Loraine looked at him and winked. "You would only know if Bone wanted you to."

Bone turned his tall Apache moccasins upside down, shook them to dislodge any nighttime occupants and pulled them on. He got to his feet after lacing them up the side.

"Coffee ready, Babe?"

Loraine lifted the lid and dumped two handfuls of Arbuckles into the boiling water. "Will be by the time you get back from taking care of your business."

"Sounds like a deal." He disappeared into the woods followed by Bear Dog.

Silke and Haven joined Tyree and Loraine at the fire.

Haven had a big smile on her face. "Ya'll are so entertainin' to listen to."

Tyree glanced at her. "You heard all that?"

"Well, of course. Neither you or Bone know how to talk softly."

"Do too."

"Do not."

"Do too."

"Do…"

"Hey!" Silke looked at them. "I'm goin' to do both of your too's, you don't shut up."

Haven stuck her tongue out at Tyree. He returned her gesture by wagging his finger at her, and then turned to the others. "Eat up, folks an' let's hit the trail. Need to get around this ridge."

Forty minutes later, Tyree led the group at a trot along the trail that circled the end of the ridge. They entered the box canyon, he held up his hand to stop, and stepped down from his saddle.

Tyree knelt at some wagon tracks in the trail.

"What do you have?" Silke also dismounted.

"Wagon tracks…headin' out an' to the north." He pointed.

Bone nudged his gelding up. "Think it's our gang with the girls?"

Tyree shook his head. "Don't know…Could be." He looked up into the canyon. "Gotta go check out the ruins in there, then we'll know…Buncha tracks, though…least six, mebe seven horses, plus the team." He remounted Laddie and headed on into the canyon.

They quickly rode past the empty lookout point and up to the abandoned cliff dwellings.

Tyree looked around. "Well, obvious they were here…"

"Were…being the operative word," interrupted Silke.

Haven glanced at Tyree. "How long since they left, you think?"

"Tracks looked a day old."

Silke grimaced, wheeled *Lakná* about, and heeled him into a lope back to the entrance. The others followed right behind her. Bear Dog ran to catch up with her.

SAN ANTONIO MOUNTAIN

The sun was well up over the horizon as Bubash refilled his cup. "What time our customers supposed to be here?"

Sterling blew across the surface of his, and then took a sip. "Boss said about noon."

"They bringing their own security?"

He nodded. "Supposed to."

"May need 'em if those Pinks show up."

Sterling glanced back up the trail. "Think you can count on it." He indicated a brown tarp covered mound next to a large boulder with his chin. "Go take a look under that tarp."

"What is it?" Bubash stepped toward the mound.

"Something the big boss left for us."

Marvin pulled the tarp aside. "What the hell is this?"

"It's called the Maxim machine gun…Used it in the Spanish American War. Shoots a .30-06 caliber bullet and has a rate of fire of over 550 rounds per minute."

"Good gosh." He looked at Sterling. "How many rounds that belt hold?"

"Two-hundred and fifty…Boss, uh…acquired it from the US Arsenal in Corpus Christi. Murphy used one in the Spanish American War."

He grinned, took out a cigar from a coat pocket, bit the end off, and lit it with a match from his vest. "Says it really chews the scenery…and anything else in front of it up." Sterling took a big draw and blew a smoke ring over his head.

Bubash chuckled and ran his hand over the smooth, polished brass surface of the four inch diameter water jacket. "Sweet."

Sterling took another draw and exhaled. "Whatever happens, we've got a Maxim machine gun…and they do not."

§§§

CHAPTER TWENTY-FIVE

BAR M RANCH

Doctor Owens pulled the stethoscope from his ears and let it hang around his neck as he stood up. "Amazing."

Luz looked over his shoulder. "What is it, Doc?"

Gentle Sky looked up at him with his dark eyes.

"Lungs are completely clear and his wounds are healing remarkably well."

Luz smiled. "Must be our lovin' care and Martina's cookin'."

"Uhh." Gentle Sky nodded. "Food good." He looked at the doctor. "Sky get up and walk? Need move around."

Doctor Owens nodded. "Don't see a problem with it, long as you don't overdo...Wouldn't want you to pull any of those stitches...Start the bleeding again."

Sky nodded.

"I'll loan him my cane...Think I can get along without it now."

They turned to see Reg Berkley standing at the door with Elizabeth. He handed the doctor the carved cedar cane.

Owens looked at Luz. "May send all my patients out here to recoup."

She raised her eyebrows. "Pass." Luz looked back at Owens. "Any news on the girls?"

He nodded. "Sheriff Russell came into town for a wagon. Said he found the girls and sent Silke an' them to where he left them. He was heading back out with the wagon."

"Saints be praised."

A look of concern flooded the big Indian's features. "Sky have trousers?"

Luz nodded and stepped over to the pine chifferobe in the corner and pulled his tan canvas pants from a drawer. "Martina washed these. 'Fraid the shirt wasn't salvageable…"

"Have clean shirt in saddlebags."

She went to the bags laying on the floor next to the chifferobe, opened one side and pulled out a large, front button, no collar, blue-striped shirt. There was a leather bound book underneath—she glanced at the hand-lettered title. *Psychotherapy in the Field* by Sigmund Freud.

Luz laid the shirt on the foot of the bed along with the trousers.

"Your moccasins are under the bed…Do you want your book?" She pulled the well-used tome from the saddlebags, held it up and cocked an eyebrow.

Sky's brown eyes widened for a brief moment, then a look of resignation crossed his face. He pursed his lips. "Well, I suppose, as Holmes would say, 'the jig is up'."

Doctor Owens, Berkley, and Luz exchanged surprised and confused glances…

SAN ANTONIO MOUNTAIN

Bubash and Sterling looked up as Ollie Wilkes led three box wagons into the clearing at the base of the mountain. There were two heavily armed gunmen with each wagon.

"Seen these fellers headed our way an' figured oughta lead 'em on in…Wouldn't want nobody gittin' shot."

Sterling nodded, pitched his cigar stub to the ground and crushed it out with the toe of his boot. "Good thinking, Wilkes…You men get down. Like some coffee?"

One of the men in a dark blue pinstriped, three piece suit, wearing a gray Homberg, stepped down from the seat of the first wagon. He removed a cheroot from his mouth. "No time. Let's get this done so we can get out of here." He looked around the area. "This place gives me the creeps."

Sterling nodded. "Whatever you say, Mister…"

He held up a finger. "Ahh, ahh, no names…You know that."

"Right…Go by numbers…1, 2, and 3." Sterling turned to Moose. "Line up the ladies right where they are against the cliff."

"Sure thing, Boss…Awright girls, on yer feet, straighten them dresses. Look nice fer the gentlemen…Gonna be 'round 'em fer a while."

Yellow Bird spat on the ground, sneered at Moose, and crossed her arms over her still developing bosom.

The man with the cheroot grinned. "Got a feisty one. Like that…Five thousand."

Sterling looked at the other buyers who had also gotten down from their wagons. They stepped forward to take a better look.

Number three raised his hand and looked at number one. "Six thousand."

The first man glared at him. "Seven."

Number three bidder grinned and shook his head declining to bid further. "Didn't want it to be too easy."

"Gate swings both ways."

VALLES CALDERA

Tyree held up his hand, and then pointed at the tracks. "Headin' through these trees toward the base of San Antonio Mountain."

Bone kneed his gelding up beside Tyree. "Suggest we spread out and go on foot from here. Looks like it's only about a quarter mile…They'll hear horses comin'."

Tyree nodded. "Agree." He looked at Silke. "Suit you?"

"Does." She dismounted and loosened *Lakná's* cinch.

Loraine and Haven did the same with Sweet Face and *d'Artagnan.* Tyree stepped down, did Laddie's girth, and then pulled the supply panniers from Ted's pack tree.

They hobbled them on some good graze after letting them water at the stream running alongside the trail.

Everyone checked their weapons. Haven strung her powerful Cheyenne war bow and slung the quiver over her back.

Silke glanced at the others. "Let's try to keep in whistling distance. I'll use a whippoorwill"

"Dove," said Haven.

"Hawk," added Bone. He looked at Loraine.

"Killdeer."

Tyree nodded. "I'll go with a cardinal."

"Let's head out. Come on Bear Dog…find." Silke pointed at the woods, then followed him into the scattered cedar.

SAN ANTONIO MOUNTAIN

The bidding was down to one left—Sarah.

"All right, that's it. Number one, you got four…two, you have three, as do you, number three. Now, if ya'll step over to our table in front of the tent…we'll settle up. Cash only, as you know." Sterling motioned to the small table with a ledger and one chair behind it. "You can have your men load your wares in your wagons."

"What about the corn silk hair girl?" Buyer number one pointed at Sarah.

"She's not available."

"The hell you say. I thought there'd be…"

"Said she's not available. The bidding is finished." Sterling glared at number one.

ANGEL JUSTICE

Jess Shepherd, the main gunhawk of Sterling's gang, stepped forward. He wore twin pearl-handled Colts in crossed gunbelts slung low on his hips. A wry smile played across his angular face.

Al Murphy took up his station behind the Maxim and racked the charging lever.

The six gunhands of the buyers looked at each other, then at their employers.

Buyer number one flexed his jaw muscles. "Wasn't the way we agreed." He turned to his men. "Load them."

His two men took his four girls and escorted them to the first box wagon. The other four did the same with their charges.

Short stairs were pulled out of the back of the wood-sided vehicles that resembled the traveling drummers wagons of the day. Each of the wagons had commercial messages lettered on the sides. One had 'Houseware', another 'Bibles', and the third, 'Doctor Good's Miracle Potion'.

The girls looked around fearfully before climbing the steps and stepping inside the dark interiors. The men closed and locked the rear doors.

The three buyers, from as far away as Denver, lined up in front of Sterling's table to pay for their newest girls of the line or fallen angels. The sales totaled $42,000.

"Everyone stay right where you are. You're surrounded. This is Deputy Sheriff Nathan Tyree of the Santa Fe County Sheriff's Department. Give it up...or face your maker an' earn your meed," a voice boomed across the clearing.

The men looked around to see Tyree standing beside a large gray boulder at the edge of the camp holding his Winchester to his shoulder, pointed in the direction of the table.

Sterling dove to the ground. "Murphy!" He scrambled for cover in some large rocks close by.

Bubash grabbed the money, then he and Sarah ducked inside the tent.

Shepherd drew both Colts and fired simultaneously at Tyree, but he was no longer there. He only got off two rounds from each pistol before an arrow appeared as if by magic at the base of his throat and extended out the back of his neck ten inches.

The hired guns scattered from the wagons, searching cover, palming their weapons as they ran.

Shepherd staggered back, dropping both pistols. He grabbed at the shaft as blood bubbled from his mouth and through his fingers. He dropped to his knees before falling to his back—dead.

The big Maxim chattered, spraying its .30-06 rounds at the prescribed rate of 500 rounds per minute. Murphy sprayed the entire area back down the trail. Noxious clouds of white gunsmoke boiled out in front of the deadly weapon.

Loraine, with her Kimber .45 semiautomatic, hunkered down behind a large ponderosa pine and double tapped Moose Welch as he raised a Greener double-barreled shotgun at Silke behind a nearby boulder. The man twisted around and dropped where he stood.

"Thanks, friend." She waved at Loraine and drew a bead on one of the guards with her Smith and Wesson 500 and squeezed the trigger.

The roar was deafening as the man's head exploded like a ripe cantaloupe being dropped from a three story building. A pink mist hung in the air a moment after he collapsed to the ground.

Bone could see just a shoulder sticking out from behind another pine. He pulled the trigger on his 500.

The 350 grain hollow point bullet caught Coon Creed's shoulder where it joined with his clavicle. The impact of the big .50 caliber round blew his shoulder, arm and all, completely from his body.

He spun around, spraying blood five feet out from his spinning body—he was dead when he hit the ground next to his arm.

Tyree noticed Haven was exposed to the deadly Maxim as Murphy raked the area. He was on the second 250 round canvas belt as the gun panned left-to-right, tearing up the trees—headed directly for her.

Tyree dove at Haven as she was drawing her bow at another of the gang, knocking her to the ground.

He rolled over after hitting her and lay still, crumpled up and limp, like a rag doll…

§§§

CHAPTER TWENTY-SIX

SAN ANTONIO MOUNTAIN

Bear Dog charged through the juniper and shinnery, leapt in the air with his one hundred and ten pounds of fury. He hit Tater Adams in the side as he levered another round into his Henry. The rifle went flying as the two forms rolled across the ground—one screaming, the other snarling.

The big wolf-dog tore at Tater's arm across his neck with his inch and a half long fangs as he tried to protect his tender throat—Bear Dog won. He ripped the man's windpipe free and slung it to the side as blood spurted in long rhythmic arches.

Bear Dog continued to maul Tater Adams for the next few seconds until he bled out and died in his jaws. He stood up and looked around for another target, blood dripping from his muzzle.

Murphy continued to pepper the area with the Maxim, now on his third ammo belt.

Bone slipped through the brush thirty yards to the side of the machine gun nest while Silke crept up from the other side an equal distance. Bone mimicked the hunting scree of a hawk.

Silke looked up and saw him on the opposite side of Murphy and answered him with the call of a whippoorwill.

Bone could barely hear it under the chatter of the Maxim and spotted her. He raised his 500, pointing at the machine gun, as Silke aimed at Murphy with her own 500. Bone made the hawk cry again and squeezed the trigger as Silke simultaneously fired hers.

The gun exploded as Bone's slug hit the receiver and set off several of the .30-06 rounds while Murphy's head disappeared in a cloud of red—the gun was silent.

Bear Dog found his next target as Ollie Wilkes ran down the entry road trying to get away. It only took a couple of seconds for him to catch and drag the outlaw down like he would if hunting and killing a deer.

Wilkes was only able to get one scream out before Bear Dog ended his life.

Loraine eased through the scattered cedar and spied Sterling crawling on his belly still trying to hide. He had a Schofield .38 in his hand. She aimed at him with a double grip.

"Far enough, scum bag."

He twisted to his right and brought the pistol to bear on Loraine.

"Mistake, ass-hat." She triple tapped his head with three shots from her .45 that sounded like one. Brain matter and chunks of skull were blown in all directions. "Told you."

She looked toward the clearing and saw three surviving gun guards and the buyers on their knees with their hands behind their heads. Silke had her

500 pointing at them as Bone walked toward Haven holding Tyree across her lap. Heavy clouds of the noxious gunsmoke still hung in the still air.

She looked up at the big man with tears in her eyes. "He took one through his side an' one through his leg. Got the bleedin' mostly stopped, but he's hurt pretty bad, Bone...Needs a doctor. He...he saved my life."

"You say both were through and through?"

Haven nodded.

"That's a good thing...if gettin' shot is ever a good thing."

He walked over to Loraine and Silke after Loraine let the girls out of the wagons. "Any sign of Sarah?"

Buyer number one spoke, "That the corn silk hair girl?"

Bone looked at the bordello owner and nodded.

"Saw her and Bubash run into the tent soon as that machine gun thing started firing."

Bone walked over and ducked through the flap at the front, his 500 still in his hand. In a short moment, he came back out.

Silke and Loraine both looked at him expectantly.

"Gone...Tent is against a cave, another lava tube...flap in the back."

"Don't have time to go lookin' for her." Silke glanced over at Haven and Tyree. "Need to get Tyree to a doctor an' these other girls back to town."

BAR M RANCH

Gentle Sky, Doctor Owens, Luz, Berkley, and Elizabeth sat out on the porch in rocking chairs. Berkley's cane lay on the floor next to Sky. He had a cup of Martina's special tea while the others had coffee. Elizabeth had a glass of her favorite, buttermilk. The sweet smell of honeysuckle drifted across the porch from the vines at the south end.

Luz shook her head and grinned. "So you're a medical doctor an' a psy...psy..."

"Psychiatrist. It's part of the medical profession, Luz. I attended the University of Paris for my medical degree and the University of Vienna to study under a man named Sigmund Freud for the new fields of psychiatry and psychoanalysis."

"So being a uneducated Indian was all an act?"

He nodded, then grinned. "Uhh."

Luz, Owens, and Berkley laughed.

"You were certainly good at it, I must say…Do we call you Doctor *Mahah* or Doctor Sky?" asked Berkley.

He smiled. "Just Sky or Gentle Sky will do…Saves a lot of explanation."

"You're probably right."

Owens nodded. "I can certainly agree with that…You're an amazing man."

"So you see why it is imperative to find Sarah?"

"I can…I can indeed." Owens sipped his coffee.

Luz pinched her lips. "If anyone can, Sky, it's Bone an' Loraine…an' Silke an' Haven…plus Nathan Tyree's no Ned in *McGuffey's Reader*."

"I'm afraid I must agree…Just wish I were along with them." He stared out across the ranch to the mountains on the east.

SAN ANTONIO MOUNTAIN

They turned at the sound of a wagon thundering along the trail coming in the direction of the clearing.

Sheriff Russell pulled back on the reins after the wagon rounded the last curve in the road, stopping the team of horses.

"Whoa! Whoa up there, boys...Ho."

The horses slid to a stop, their sides heaving, necks lathered and blowing slobber from their mouths. Dust boiled up behind them.

"Heard all the gunfire an' figured had to be ya'll...So I cut this way." He glanced around at the bodies and the girls standing, holding each other. "What happened here?"

Ten minutes later, they had filled the sheriff in on everything that had happened.

"One of the girls..." Silke nodded at Sally Ann.

"Said the missing man is a Marvin Bubash, an' is the one who disappeared with Sarah into the tent with the money, an' apparently on into the tube."

"So no one has gone in there lookin' for her?" asked the sheriff.

"Went in far as the light would let us when we took the tent down...Nothing," said Bone. "We have to get Tyree to the doc."

Russell looked at the dark foreboding opening. "Ya'll go ahead on to town with him, the girls an' the prisoners. I'll stay, make some torches, an' go in there…My team is purty played out an' got to have some rest, anyways."

"By yourself?" asked Silke.

Russell looked askance at her.

She nodded. "Right."

"Evil live there."

They turned to see who was talking. It was Yellow Bird.

"*Yee naaldooshii* here."

"What's that?" Haven looked puzzled.

The sheriff turned to her. "Means Skinwalker…the Navajo boogie man."

"Shapeshifters are all over the world…and have been since the first civilizations, Sheriff."

He smiled. "Not much difference between religion an' superstition, Bone."

"Not going to argue that point, Sheriff, but we've already seen some things in this caldera we can't explain." He glanced at Silke and the others.

"The eyes can see a lot of things the mind can't get a hold of or explain…Don't mean they're spirits or Skinwalkers…just things we didn't get a good look at...As a law officer, you know how we have to handle so-called *eye witnesses*." He smiled.

"Got a point, there, too...Up to you, stay and look." Bone turned to Loraine. "Babe, why don't you redress Tyree's wounds, put plenty of alum powder on 'em so they don't start bleeding again on the trip...Silke, you and Haven put that folded up tent and some of the blankets they had in one of those box wagons to make a bed for him. Try to pad it up much as you can."

"That's a good idea, Bone. Come on Haven let's do it."

Haven gently laid Tyree's head down and got to her feet.

Loraine looked over at the girls. "Sally, you and Yellow Bird give me a hand, would you?"

"Yes, Ma'am," they said together and moved over to where Tyree lay.

Bone waved his 500 at the three buyers and the three remaining guards still on their knees with their hands behind their heads. "You three upstanding citizens are going to drive two of the wagons to Santa Fe. Our wounded deputy will be in one, the girls in another and the bodies in the third."

Buyer number one protested. "We need to get back to our own cities."

Bone chuckled. "Not going to happen, sunshine. You broke the law...or didn't you know kidnapping an' slavery was illegal?...Both are felonies."

"We didn't kidnap anyone. We..."

"Ever hear of accessory...before and after the fact?...The judge will explain it to you right before he passes sentence...Twenty to thirty years in Leavenworth or I miss my guess."

Bone looked at the three gunmen. "You three are going to collect all the bodies...after I gather up the weapons. You'll put them in that wagon." He pointed. "And you get to ride in the back with them."

"But those are woodsided wagons, there's no ventilation," complained one of the gunmen.

Bone cocked his head and grinned. "Do tell? You're breakin' my heart, babycakes...Now get to it." He waved his hand cannon at them.

Sheriff Russell glanced at Bone directing the prisoners and a wry smile flashed briefly across his face as he unhooked his team of horses to take

them to water before building some torches and
starting his search of the cave…

§§§

EPILOGUE

VALLES CALDERA

Buyer number one drove the first wagon carrying Tyree. Haven rode in the bed with him holding his hand with her blue roan gelding, *d'Artagnan*, tied to the back as Silke led the way on *Lakná*. Bear

Dog trotted alongside them. Tyree's Laddie was also tied at the back.

Bone had removed the wood panels from the side to make it an open wagon. He did the same with the second wagon carrying the girls, driven by buyer number two with Ted tied to the tailgate. The third, with buyer three, hauling the bodies and the three hired guns, was left intact, much to the chagrin of the gunhawks.

Bone and Loraine rode behind the column as they headed toward Santa Fe.

SAN ANTONIO MOUNTAIN

Sheriff Russell staked the team out on some graze before he made up two torches. He used a couple of limbs he picked up, wrapped one end in some burlap he carried to rub down the horses and coated the material with pine sap from a nearby tree.

He lit one of the torches with a match from his vest and stepped inside the dark ancient lava tube. The sheriff held the torch closer to the floor of the cave and could easily make out two sets of footprints in the dust—one set was small.

Case moved deeper into the prehistoric lava tube, occasionally checking the tracks. He froze. Abruptly, another set of tracks appeared on top of Sarah and Bubash's—the tracks of a giant wolf. He looked from side to side and back a few steps—no wolf tracks.

Russell shook his head in disbelief. *No way they just suddenly appeared...but they did.* He held the torch closer to the floor as he moved forward—then he froze again.

Just ahead was a body lying in the middle of the tube. He rushed forward and knelt down bedside Sarah and felt her face. Her eyes fluttered, then opened.

"Who?"

"It's me, honey. Are you hurt?"

Sarah raised up on one elbow. "Don't think so." She looked around in a panic. "Where is it?"

"What?"

Sarah looked around again. "The creature...it was just here...and where's Mason?"

"Who?"

"The man...He had the money."

"Bubash." Russell held his torch up a little and looked around the floor. Bubash's tracks and those of the giant wolf completely disappeared—along with the satchel of cash.

He held the torch higher and looked deeper into the tube. There was a brief flash of a set of red eyes over six feet above the floor of the cave, then they disappeared. Russell stared into the darkness of the shaft for a few more moments, his hand on the butt of his Colt before he turned and helped Sarah to her feet.

"Let's get out of here."

They headed back toward the entrance. The sheriff's first torch was sputtering and went out as they walked into the daylight.

He looked down at her dirt smeared face. "Are you awright, honey?"

Sarah blinked against the bright light. "I think so."

Suddenly she threw her arms about his neck. "Oh, thank you, Daddy, thank you." She sobbed against his broad chest.

"It's awright now, honey, you're safe."

She shook her head and looked up at him. "No we're not…not till we're away from this awful place."

He led her over to a large rock. "You sit here while I get the horses and hook 'em up to the wagon."

"No! Don't leave me alone. I'll go with you."

He nodded and led her to where he had left the picketed horses to graze.

They were standing, stomping their front feet, snorting, and staring in the direction of the cave entrance.

Sheriff Russell and Sarah turned and looked behind them—they saw nothing. They turned back as the two horses squealed and reared up, pawing the air with their front feet.

The sheriff and Sarah spun back around. Both screamed. Russell drew his Colt and fired three rounds—then there was total silence…

VALLES CALDERA

Silke reined *Lakná* around and galloped back to Bone and Loraine.

"Hear that?"

Bone nodded. "Sounded like gunshots coming from back at the mountain. Watch our friends, we'll go check it out."

He and Loraine wheeled their mounts around and kicked them into a gallop in the direction of the camp. It was almost five miles. Bear Dog loped in their wake.

SAN ANTONIO MOUNTAIN

Ten minutes later they had slowed Hildebrandt and Sweet Face to a lope as they rode into the clearing at the cave.

They quickly dismounted and moved toward the nervous team horses, still stomping their front feet and snorting.

Bear Dog froze as the hair on his hackles stood erect and a growl rumbled from his throat.

"Look." Loraine walked forward and picked up a stag-handled Colt. "This is Sheriff Russell's." She pulled the hammer to half-cock and rotated the cylinder. "Three fired." She smelled the barrel and nodded. "Recently."

Bone knelt and studied the ground. "His tracks and Sarah's coming from the cave..." He looked up at Loraine. "Giant wolf tracks."

Bear Dog smelled the tracks and growled again followed by a low whine.

Loraine looked around the area. "They don't go anywhere."

Bear Dog turned and looked at the cave.

Bone nodded. "They just disappear."

VALLES CALDERA

Bone and Loraine trotted up to the three wagons. He was leading Sheriff Russell's two horses.

Silke trotted forward to meet them. "What was it?"

Bone shook his head. "Nobody there. Found the sheriff and Sarah's tracks along with his pistol..."

"Been fired three times," interrupted Loraine.

"They were gone...Just gone...Like the Anasazi."

Silke glanced around the area a little nervously and adjusted her Smith and Wesson in its holster.

Yellow Bird and Moon Water could hear the conversation as they looked at one another, nodded, and both their lips mouthed, *"Yee naaldooshii."* The other Navajo in the wagon as well as the Apache, also nodded.

SANTA FE

Silke pulled rein at the Sheriff's Office adobe building and dismounted. Bone and Loraine followed suit. Silke went inside while Bone and Loraine stayed out with the prisoners.

Sheriff Russell had left a young deputy, Red Gibson, to run the jail and make rounds. He was called 'Red' for obvious reasons.

"Miss Silke, you're back." He got to his feet.

"Could say that. Got some prisoners for you and some bodies for the county coroner. Plus need the doc for Deputy Tyree…Now!…We'll get the prisoners locked up while you run get the doc. You can book these miscreants when you get back with him…That all right?"

"Yessum." He shot to his feet and rushed out the door.

She stepped to the still open doorway and motioned to Bone and Loraine to bring the prisoners inside.

Bone unlatched the rear door of the wagon with the gunmen while Loraine got the three buyers lined up on the boardwalk.

"Now you boys don't do anything stupid and I won't have to sic my sweet wife here, on you...she'll hurtcha. Trust me on that."

Loraine grinned. "Now you jugheads, inside." She pointed at the open doorway where Silke stood.

Bone looked over in the wagon with Tyree and Haven. "How's he doing?"

Haven looked up, she still held his hand as she had done all the way into town. "He's been in an' out. Moaned some over the rougher places but he's some kinda tough." She caressed the side of his face with her other hand.

His eyes fluttered as he looked up at her. "Am I dead?"

"No, silly, why do you ask that?"

He frowned a little. "Aren't...aren't you an angel?" His eyes closed again.

"Oh…" She turned her head so he wouldn't see the tears filling her eyes.

Red came up the walk with Doctor Owens carrying his black bag. Bone dropped the tailgate to the wagon.

"Figured you wanted to look at him in the wagon first before you decide where to put him."

"Good thinking, Bone." He looked at Haven. "He been awake any?"

She nodded. "Off an' on."

He eased the blanket off the top of his chest and listened to his lungs and heart with his stethoscope. "Hmm…That's good."

A concerned Haven glanced up. "What's good?"

He smiled. "No blood in his airways, heart's slow but steady. Help me get these bandages away from the wounds."

Bone turned to the young deputy. "Red, need you to make a list of the girls and go to the telegram office and send what telegrams you can, then hire whoever you need to find all their folks and tell 'em to come get their children."

"You bet, Deputy Bone." He took a notepad from his pocket and stepped up into the back of the girl's wagon.

After the doctor had inspected the wounds, Haven assisted him in redressing them. Tyree woke up several times, looked at Doctor Owens in some confusion and dropped back off.

"Think we should take him on out to Luz's..." He grinned. "Best clinic around...I'll stitch him up out there where I can do it proper." He looked over at Bone, Loraine, Silke, and Haven. "Sky has made a remarkable recovery...and you literally won't believe what else."

Bone wrinkled his brow. "What do you mean?"

"I'll let him tell you. You won't see any of it...and I mean any, coming."

BAR M RANCH

Night had settled as everyone had dragged chairs into Tyree's room. He was propped up on several pillows against the headboard, his chest was wrapped in bandages and Haven was feeding him some of Martina's bone broth.

Gentle Sky was in the same rocker he had sat in out on the porch—all eyes were on the big Indian. There were smiles on Luz, Berkley, and Doctor Owens because they already knew what was coming.

"Sky, are you going to tell us the rest or do you and I have to tussle again…Might be different with you being still a bit stove up."

Sky grinned at Bone. "Give me a couple of weeks on that." He looked around the room. "As I told Luz and them earlier, gold had been discovered on our tribal lands and nothing would suit my mother more than I become a doctor. I had already gone as far with my education as I could locally and at Oklahoma A & M in Stillwater." He took a sip of his tea. "My counselor arranged for me to attend the University of Paris."

"You got to travel to Paris…in France?" questioned Haven.

He smiled again. "Certainly not Paris, Texas, child."

They all laughed. Haven blushed and squeezed Tyree's hand.

My best friend back home had married and gave birth to a child while I was in Paris. I came home for a visit and she and I noticed some aberrant behavior in the little girl at the age of two."

Everyone but Luz, Berkley, and Doctor Owens exchanged glances.

"Aberrant?"

Doctor Owens glanced at Haven. "Diverging from normal behavior."

"Oh."

"I had heard of a Doctor Sigmund Freud in Vienna and his studies in psychoanalysis."

Haven frowned again. "Psycho…Never mind."

"So I studied for the next year with Doctor Freud and came back home."

"Was the child still exhibiting abnormal behavior?" asked Loraine.

Sky nodded. "Even more ingrained…And to make matters worse, my friend, her mother, contracted cholera and passed away. All my training couldn't help her. Her father, Case Russell…"

There were several sharp intakes of breath around the room.

Silke nodded. "Another one of her lies that she was Wilford's daughter."

"Correct…Well, Case, asked me to be Sarah's nanny, so to speak, and do what I could for her. There was nothing Case wouldn't do for Sarah. She could twist him around her finger…so, we decided to send her to a boarding school…I went with her, of course."

Bone cocked his head. "What was the diagnosis of her behavior?"

Sky paused for a long moment. "I determined, after some long distance consultation with Doctor Freud that she was a classic Psychopathic Sociopath."

Silke held up her hand. "In English."

Sky took a deep breath. "A manipulative person, seen by others as charming, able to lead a semblance of a normal life but with a personality disorder manifesting itself in extreme antisocial attitudes and behavior…And with a complete lack of conscience…by definition."

"I said in English."

"She has no concept of right or wrong and will do anything…lie, cheat, steal, or kill…to achieve her goals with no semblance of guilt."

Silke nodded. "So she manipulated her father, Sheriff Case Russell, to set up a sex slave ring for what purpose?"

Sky pursed his lips. "Near as I can figure…for power and money. She wanted to control others lives…Sarah was just evil, pure evil."

Haven shook her head. "I don't understand why she allowed herself to be kidnapped as one of the potential slaves…almost getting you killed in the process."

"I believe she wanted an inside look, for a thrill…I was just collateral damage. No one knew who she was, except her father. He was doing all the leg work…posing as the boss but she was the controlling factor."

"I was on the verge of being able to shut her down and finally convince her it wasn't the thing to do…" Sky looked off.

Silke looked at Bone. "And they just vanished outside that cave with the giant wolf tracks?"

"So it would seem, Silke, so it would seem."

Tyree looked around the room and spoke softly, "Skinwalkers took them…Evil with evil."

§§§§§

PREVIEW

OF THE NEXT

EXCITING
KEN FARMER NOVEL

SKINWALKER JUSTICE

CHAPTER ONE

VALLES CALDERA

A set of glowing red eyes peered out of the inky depths of the ancient lava tube at the young couple. They had halted their team of mules hooked to a covered wagon at a clearing below the cave.

The sandy-haired twenty-four year old man clambered down from the seat, turned around and assisted his attractive blonde wife of one week to the ground.

"I'll go gather some wood for a fire before I unhook the team, dear."

She batted her blue eyes at him. "Thank you, my love. I'll get some supper started then."

William and Mary Lou Greene had been married in Santa Fe last week. They were headed to their new home in Phoenix, Arizona to take over a general mercantile purchased for them by her father.

They had stopped the team at the west ridge of the fourteen mile wide depression in the New Mexico landscape. The depression, known as the Valles Caldera was formed in the Pleistocene when a giant volcano collapsed into its empty magma chamber.

The entire area was honeycombed with caves and empty lava tubes. The local Navajo Indians avoided it as they considered it an evil place and a home to the *Yeenaaldooshii*—the Skinwalkers or shapeshifters.

It was a Navajo legend that evil spirits could take physical form, most often that of the prehistoric giant predator known as the Dire

Wolf—extinct for the last ten thousand years. William and Mary Lou were unaware of this legend.

William staked the mules out on some good graze after pulling their harness and leading them down to the nearby stream for water.

Gloaming had settled on the caldera as Mary Lou stirred the skillet of canned meat mixed with a can of beans for their supper.

"Coffee ready, dear?"

She glanced up at him, with a look that only newlyweds have. "It's all ready, boiled twice like mama taught me."

He squatted down, grabbed the blue speckled graniteware pot with his folded over glove and filled his cup. William blew across the top to cool it down, licked the rim, and took a sip of the very bitter liquid.

Mary Lou looked over at him with a big expectant grin. "How is it?"

William cleared his throat. "Mmm, mmm, mama's got nothin' on this, sweetie." He crossed his fingers behind his back with his other hand to offset his perfidious statement.

"Why, thank you, dearest."

The twilight quickly turned to a moonless darkness with the only light coming from the flickering fire.

Night sounds of frogs, crickets, cicadas, and birds seeking a roost filled the area—then all abruptly stopped.

SANTA FE SHERIFF'S OFFICE

The sun approached noon apogee as Silke, Haven, Bone, and Loraine sat in the front office of the adobe building housing the sheriff's office and jail. They were nursing their third cup of coffee.

Silke's black, blue-eyed, half wolf, Bear Dog, snored peacefully in front of the potbellied stove.

Bone, as the senior law enforcement officer, was appointed acting sheriff while Deputy Nathan Tyree continued healing from the two gunshot wounds he had suffered.

It would be two months before an election could be held to replace Sheriff Case Russell who had disappeared in the Valles Caldera along with his fifteen year old daughter recently.

SKINWALKER JUSTICE

The psychotic sociopathic daughter, Sarah, and her father, but mostly Sarah, had masterminded a Red sex slave ring that Silke, along with Haven, Bone, Loraine, and Tyree—with a little help from Bear Dog—had shut down and rescued eleven teenage girls from the living hell of going to bordellos.

The strawberry blonde Silke looked around the room at the others. "Be dang glad when Tyree gets healed up enough to take over this sheriffin'...Tendin' toward bein' borin'."

Bone grinned. "Name of the game, Silke...Either you're covered up or you sit around doing nothing."

Silke's look-alike eighteen year old, sable-haired cousin, Haven, let her chair back forward and set her empty cup on the desk. "Could have Gentle Sky teach us how to play chess like he's doin' Tyree."

"We can show ya'll how to play bridge. Four can play that card game," said Loraine.

Haven looked at the attractive police detective of Mexican descent who held a seventh degree black belt in Kung Fu. "What's bridge?"

She cocked an eyebrow. "It evolved from the British game of Whist…but it's better."

"How better?"

A farmer in blue striped overalls over a boiled once white cotton shirt and wearing a battered straw hat burst into the room. Bear Dog shot to his feet growling at the intruder.

"Bear Dog, down," commanded Silke.

"Deputy Bone, ya'll gotta come."

Bone got to his feet. "What is it and who are you?"

The farmer jerked his hat from his head. "Name's Buckwilder, Cletus Buckwilder an' ya'll gotta come."

"All right, get that part, Cletus. Gotta come where?"

"Take a breath, calm down a bit," said Silke.

He nodded. "Yessum…Was headin' to my place on the other side of the caldera an' went past a campsite down by the creek. Recognized the Greene's wagon. Seen 'em leave town yest'day. They's newlyweds."

Bone frowned. "And?"

"Their camp was torn all to hell…Beg pardon, ladies."

"Heard worse, continue," commented Silke.

"Like I said, camp torn all to hell...an' the kids was gone."

Bone looked askance at him. "Gone?"

"Yessir...Gone. Not a trace. All their stuff just scattered about."

Loraine glanced at Bone, then back at Cletus. "Did you see any blood or anything?"

He shook his head. "Uh-uh, nothin' Ma'am...They's just gone."

Everyone exchanged glances...

§§§

OTHER NOVELS FROM
TIMBER CREEK PRESS
www.timbercreekpress.net

MILITARY ACTION/TECHNO

BLACK EAGLE FORCE: Eye of the Storm (Book #1)
by Buck Stienke and Ken Farmer

BLACK EAGLE FORCE: Sacred Mountain (Book #2) by Buck Stienke and Ken Farmer

RETURN of the STARFIGHTER (Book #3)
by Buck Stienke and Ken Farmer

BLACK EAGLE FORCE: BLOOD IVORY (Book #4)
by Buck Stienke and Ken Farmer with Doran Ingrham

BLACK EAGLE FORCE: FOURTH REICH (Book #5) by Buck Stienke and Ken Farmer

AURORA: INVASION (Book #6 in the BEF) by Ken Farmer & Buck Stienke

BLACK EAGLE FORCE: ISIS (Book #7) by Buck Stienke and Ken Farmer

BLOOD BROTHERS - Doran Ingrham, Buck Stienke and Ken Farmer

DARK SECRET - Doran Ingrham

NICARAGUAN HELL - Doran Ingrham

BLACKSTAR BOMBER by T.C. Miller

BLACKSTAR BAY by T.C. Miller

BLACKSTAR MOUNTAIN by T.C. Miller
BLACKSTAR ENIGMA by T.C. Miller

HISTORICAL FICTION WESTERN
THE NATIONS by Ken Farmer and Buck Stienke
HAUNTED FALLS by Ken Farmer and Buck Stienke
HELL HOLE by Ken Farmer
ACROSS the RED by Ken Farmer and Buck Stienke
BASS and the LADY by Ken Farmer and Buck Stienke
DEVIL'S CANYON by Buck Stienke
LADY LAW by Ken Farmer
BLUE WATER WOMAN by Ken Farmer
FLYNN by Ken Farmer
AURALI RED by Ken Farmer
COLDIRON by Ken Farmer
STEELDUST by Ken Farmer
BONE by Ken Farmer
BONE'S LAW by Ken Farmer
BONE & LORAINE by Ken Farmer
BONE'S GOLD by Ken Farmer
BONE'S ENIGMA by Ken Farmer
SILKE JUSTICE by Ken Farmer
SILKE'S QUEST by Ken Farmer
NO TIME to DIE by Buck Stienke

SILKE'S RIDE by Ken Farmer
ANGEL JUSTICE by Ken Farmer

SY/FY
LEGEND of AURORA by Ken Farmer & Buck Stienke
AURORA: INVASION (Book #6 in the BEF) by Ken Farmer & Buck Stienke

HISTORICAL FICTION ROMANCE
THE TEMPLAR TRILOGY
MYSTERIOUS TEMPLAR by Adriana Girolami
THE CRIMSON AMULET by Adriana Girolami
TEMPLAR'S REDEMPTION by Adriana Girolami

MYSTERY
BONE'S PARADOX by Buck Stienke
THE LOCK BOX by Terry D. Heflin

CIVIL WAR ROMANACE
SCARLET HEM by Terry D. Heflin

Coming Soon

HISTORICAL FICTION WESTERN
McGRATH by T.C. Miller
SKINWALKER JUSTICE by Ken Farmer

CIVIL WAR ROMANCE
GOLDEN CIRCLE by Terry D. Heflin

HISTORICAL FICTION ROMANCE
DAUGHTER of HADES by Adriana Girolami
ZAMINDAR and the LADY by Adriana Girolami

SY/FY
ANTAREAN DILEMMA by T.C. Miller

MYSTERY
RECIPE for MURDER by Ken Farmer & Buck Stienke

Thanks for reading *ANGEL JUSTICE.* If you enjoyed it, I would really appreciate a review on Amazon.

You may contact me at pagact@yahoo.com
My FaceBook Page:
www.facebook.com/KenFarmerAuthor/
Amazon Author Page:
www.amazon.com/Ken-Farmer/e/B0057OT3YI

TIMBER CREEK PRESS

www.ingramcontent.com/pod-product-compliance
Lightning Source LLC
Chambersburg PA
CBHW020223260626
47156CB00002B/507